I0565980

River:
A
Vampire's
Nightmare

GARY LEE VINCENT

Burning Bulb
PUBLISHING

River: A Vampire's Nightmare
By **Gary Lee Vincent**

Burning Bulb Publishing
P.O. Box 4721
Bridgeport, WV 26330-4721
United States of America
www.BurningBulbPublishing.com

PUBLISHER'S NOTE: This book is a work of fiction. Names, characters, places, and incidents are either the product of the author's imagination or are used fictitiously, and any resemblance to actual persons, living or dead, events, or locales is purely coincidental.

Copyright © 2020 Gary Lee Vincent. All rights reserved.

Cover designed by Gary Lee Vincent with a background photo by Vlad Bagacian from Pexels augmented with an image from NightCafe.

First Edition.

Paperback Edition ISBN: 978-1-948278-25-6

Dedicated to
Michelle Bowser

BOOK 1
A VAMPIRE'S NIGHTMARE

CHAPTER 1

River & Ivy

Thursday at midnight.

Party sounds throbbed up through the floor of one of the penthouse bedrooms of the Haven nightclub.

Douglas River, both the bedroom's owner and the club's manager, stood naked by one of its windows staring out across the Morgantown skyline.

Behind him in the bedroom's triple bed, a slim blonde woman watched his muscular back. The woman, Ivy Rain, was quite stoned. While studying River's pleasing rear view, she languidly smoked a joint. Occasionally she took her eyes off of her lover to regard the trails of marijuana smoke she was puffing into the air.

"Come back to bed and let's do it again," she told River's back.

He shook his head without turning. "In a little bit, baby. I'm getting a good feeling here."

She giggled and dragged on her joint again. "I've got something warm here for you to feel. I'm certain my body will feel a whole lot better against yours than the cold wind does." Then, when he showed no sign of leaving the window, she seemed to forget him. In the week she'd been living with him, Ivy had grown used to River's coldness.

For his part, River had already forgotten his house guest, expelling her from his mind and once again letting the city in. The Haven nightclub was situated in the northeast sector of town, on Easton Mill Road, which was near the Municipal Airport. It was surrounded by trees, but from the penthouse one had a relatively unobstructed view of the city.

River let Morgantown seep into him in incremental stages: its lights, its decadences (as evidenced by the noises of reveling coming from the ground floor), and its delightful smell of warm bodies and the much warmer blood those bodies all contained.

River smiled. He was a vampire, and to a vampire the smell of human blood always brought intense pleasure. Smelling humans, he was a predator smelling food.

But then he felt the headache again—a splitting pain like a nail being driven into his left temple—and the decadent predatory smirk instantly wiped off his face.

And once again, just as had happened yesterday, along with the headache came the 'reversal,' as he now thought of it: for a painfully stretched-out moment his senses seemed to invert themselves and the blood stink he'd previously reveled in and which had filled his mouth with hungry expectant saliva and made his fangs extend out from his upper jaw, vanished from his mind and what filled it instead was disgust at the urge to drink blood, and the desire to retch—a feeling of drowning in a red river, of being swept away on a raging tide of liquid nastiness.

For those moments he felt disgusted with himself, with who he was. With what he was. Trying to put his finger on it, River imagined he felt the way one of his human victims did right before he sank his fangs into them and sucked their delicious red life out.

For that long moment, River stood paralyzed by the window, his eyes closed, bracing himself against the windowsill so he didn't fall forward out of it.

The moment passed. The raging pain in his head dissolved. Just like that his discomfort and inversion of desires was over.

He opened his eyes and frowned. Once certain he'd keep his balance, he removed his hand from the windowsill and felt himself. His body felt normal—cool as a snake's. He was glad he'd not toppled out of the window. The three-floor fall to the parking lot wouldn't have hurt him, but naked as he was, it was certain to be embarrassing getting back into the building and upstairs.

What the hell is happening to me? What in Hades' name is going on?

With no answers to that question, and needing some distraction, he remembered he wasn't alone in the bedroom and turned to face his house guest.

River had never had any problems attracting women. He was a handsome, dark and debonair man, with a slight cleft in the chin that enhanced his old-school kind of masculine appeal. One or two associates of his had even said he resembled the old-time actor Vincent Price. Though he was now a hundred and twenty-five years old, outwardly he looked only thirty-five. The one clue to River's true age were his eyes, which, in addition to giving him an aura of jaded wisdom, were also as cold as ice, projecting no emotion whatever, though they did occasionally reveal his hunger when he sighted human prey

But if River's blue eyes were as cold as ice, they nevertheless seemed to promise his potential lovers wicked and forbidden thrills; taboo-like ecstasies. It didn't hurt that he ran a successful nightclub. The women wanted parties and excitement, they wanted danger. Drink and drugs too.

But most of all, the women who came to Douglas River wanted darkness—they sensed a jaded evil in him and wanted a taste of it. Too bad that for some of the women that taste would prove fatal. Once a woman had her first taste of vampire it just might be her last.

Like this one, for instance. Ivy Rain. She was a dancer—a stripper. She'd come to the club looking for work, but Haven wasn't a strip joint. Instead of hitting the road again though, she'd given River that 'come hither' look and then given him a private lap dance, after which he'd moved her into his penthouse suite. She'd been living with him for a week now.

Ivy noticed she had his attention again. She waved at him through her marijuana haze. "Miss me yet?" she asked, pointing to his penis. "Your dick looks all cold from standing by the window. Come to me, baby, let me warm it up a li'l bit."

He climbed onto the huge bed.

Ivy was in her early thirties. Pretty, with white-blonde hair and a knockout body. She smiled coolly at him as he approached her. She had several bite marks on her neck. He'd bitten her on the second day, just as she'd been about to orgasm, and rather than flee in horror she'd become addicted to the feeling.

She was one of those people who grew attracted to the darkness; or rather the fictional beauty of the darkness; and like a naïve moth drawn to a negative flame, she was powerless to curb her intense attraction to death before it consumed and killed her.

"Will I become a vampire too?" she'd asked afterwards, not actually believing he was one either, but playing along with the joke because him biting her and drinking her blood stimulated her jaded senses. And besides, after their affair ended and she moved on, she'd have another anecdote to tell her stripper friends. He felt he could read her decadent life in her eyes. She'd grown tired of everyday thrills.

"No," he'd joked as answer to her question. "For you to become like me, you'd have to die first."

"Live, die, undie." She'd shook her head. "Sounds painful, baby. Me, I like me just the way I am."

He'd laughed coldly. "I do too." Then he'd bitten her again.

He'd been careful to drink just a little of Ivy's blood each time they fucked. But even that little had had its effect. Her soporific state now wasn't entirely the result of the marijuana she was smoking. Unknown and unnoticed by Ivy herself, she'd been growing more and more lethargic during their week together, her energy draining away along with her blood. For the past two days, she'd been too enervated to even descend to the ground floor restaurant to eat; he'd had her meals brought up to her and even then she'd only picked at the food, preferring to get high and make love, which had to always climax with him biting her again.

Now as he moved on hands and knees towards the prone blonde, a desperate fire seemed to flicker in her blue eyes. After pinching out her joint, she reached eagerly for him. As eagerly as though *she* were the predator here and not himself.

Surely she must suspect her fate, he thought in some amusement as she sucked his fast-stiffening penis into her mouth. *She just has no idea of how painful it's gonna be.*

And then River gave himself up to the pleasures of the flesh. Sex was one of the few pleasures a vampire had. With their altered metabolisms, most drugs didn't get them high, and even their craving for blood was more like a heroin addict's need for a regular fix than anything else. Sure, it was great to live at the top of the food chain, but the price was a living hell.

Ivy was very good in bed. As she sucked his erection, her fingers stroked the spit-wet length. River found himself able to forget the awful headaches and reversals he'd been experiencing. He let himself go, while she fellated him lustily. Sensing himself about to ejaculate, he roughly pushed her face off his member.

She looked up at him expectantly.

"Lie on your belly," he said.

She rolled over and parted her legs. He lay on her; his pale body on her tan one. She gasped as he slipped into her from behind, then pushed herself up to meet him. Faster and faster they moved together, his cold body on her warm one; his cold organ (though he knew Ivy was too far gone now to notice that) inside her warm one.

"Bite, me, darling!" she gasped as she began to come. "Bite me deep."

Feeling his own orgasm coming too, he sank his fangs deep into her neck. This time he didn't drink just a little of her. He drank deeply, loving the thrill of her essence rushing into him even as his sperm rushed out into her body.

She gasped through her orgasm, her body shaking from the mix of pleasure and pain she was feeling. Afterwards, she rolled on her back and gazed at him in wonder. Two thin lines of blood dribbled from the latest two holes in her neck.

"That was fantastic," she told River with affection in her eyes, her little breasts heaving with each word. "Just now I felt like I was dying." She reached out a hand and stroked his chest.

He smiled, leaned over and licked the blood trickles from her neck, then replied, "It was great for me too, honey. While fucking you, I felt like I was really living."

And it had been great. The sex had shunted his recent worries about the headaches to the rear of the queue of his concerns.

Now, while staring nicely at Ivy, he decided it was time to introduce her to the horrors of the nightclub's basement. By her own admission she was itinerant. Originally from Indianapolis, she'd arrived here in West Virginia by way of Ohio, when she hadn't liked any of the strip joints she'd auditioned for. Personal-effects-wise, Ivy had two suitcases and her battered Ford Fiesta which was parked out back. When she disappeared as River intended her to, no one would look for her. He'd have Tasha, one of the club's vampire employees, dress up in Ivy's clothes and drive her Ford to a vampire garage in Westover for disposal. End of trail. End of Ivy Rain.

But not immediately, first he needed to put in an appearance at the party downstairs. Ivy, her arms spread out by her sides, had fallen asleep. A little more blood had seeped from the fresh punctures in her throat. Not wanting to wake her, he resisted the urge to suck at them again.

Suddenly River's skin felt sticky and unpleasant. He got out of bed and went to have a shower.

As he stood soaping himself under the hot spray, with clouds of steam billowing around him, he sped his mind forward over the coming week's activities.

Most important was the visit of the vampire head, Max King. King and his daughter Alexia, who were currently touring the east coast, would be arriving from Richmond, VA tomorrow night. Seeing as the Haven nightclub was the number one spot for West Virginia's vampire nightlife, River would be playing host to the vampire leader. It was a heady responsibility. River was ambitious. He'd wanted to get into Max King's good books for ages. Now that he had his opportunity to make a favorable impression on the head vampire he wasn't about to trivialize or waste it.

The thought of Max King's arrival galvanized River. There was work to be done. The adjoining penthouse suites needed to be prepared for occupancy. Above all, he needed to ensure there was sufficient fresh blood in their fridges.

Max King was known to have a partiality to the blood of virgins. River would see if he could locate some. It might prove hard though: except for prepubescent girls (and to avoid police investigations, the vampires tended to leave kids alone) and Catholic school students (where all the holy relics on display made prospecting a no-no), virgins were in really short supply nowadays.

While toweling himself off, River mused on King's culinary preference. Personally, he'd never detected any difference between the flavor of the blood of virgins or deflowered women. But apparently Max King, who seemed as old as Satan himself, and who'd come over from the Old Country ages ago in a wooden box packed with Transylvanian soil, could differentiate between them. King had apparently been best friends with Dracula himself before that asshole Van Helsing staked old Vlad one time too many.

There was plenty of blood at the BSS clinic. Although ran under the auspice of a standard blood bank for the local hospitals, it was ran by the vampire syndicate as a source of fresh blood and other 'services' when required by their nocturnal patrons.

Usually, he'd simply delegate the job of procuring some to Tasha or his assistant night manager Pale Joe to handle. Problem was, Pale Joe might intentionally screw him over and order hag's blood instead. And Max King was known to *abhor* hag's blood. It was said to be what he'd been drinking the first time a vampire hunter had almost staked him. It was also said that up till that moment, he'd been enjoying himself greatly, as the hag in question was his mother-in-law.

River left the bathroom. As he entered his bedroom, Ivy sat up, her whitish hair scattered around her face. Now, as she stared at him, her expression was an uncertain one. She seemed scared, as if she'd had a premonition or two about him during her short doze.

She sat there looking like she'd cut and run if she could find sufficient energy to do so. He decided it was time to dispose of her. Then he'd join the party downstairs and also focus his attentions on getting things ready for tomorrow's visit by the vampire elite.

"Get dressed, baby," he said, crossing to his closet. "We're going downstairs."

She shook her head at him. "To the club? Man, I don't think I can handle that right now. Maybe it's all the blood you've been sucking outa me, but I feel weak as hell. Like I need to sleep forever, or"—her gaze left him and moved instead to the nightstand holding the ashtray where she'd placed the remains of her last joint—"Or, like I need to get high again."

He paused in buttoning up his shirt and shook his head at her. "We ain't going to the club, darling. I've got a great surprise for you in the basement."

She looked surprised. "This place has a basement?"

He laughed at how naïve she was. "Of course it does, Ivy. It's where we vampires drain all the blood from our victim's corpses." He pulled on his pants. "Like you, for instance. There's only so much blood I can suck out of you. No matter how hard I try, I can only drain about half of what you've got inside those lovely blood vessels of yours. But downstairs we've modern machines that'll empty you completely."

"You're joking, right?" Ivy asked. Now she began really looking scared. It wasn't his words that had her terrified, but the nasty look in his eyes. A pitiless look, like that of a wolf staring at dinner. She'd gone along with all the blood play, it had been fun, but now . . . seeing him lick his teeth at her, she felt terrified at what was about to happen to her.

He shook his head at her. "Not at all, honey. Your time's up. Your life is over. I'm through with you."

"I can just leave," she pleaded. "It'll be like I was never here."

He watched in amusement as she slowly inched her way along the bed towards the bedroom door, trying to making a run for it. "Either way, It'll be as if you were never here."

She leapt up off the bed then. But moving at a speed that astounded her, he was already in front of the bedroom door waiting for her. She turned to dash away, but he grabbed her around the waist, pulled her strongly back and turned her to face him again. She kicked and struggled to get free, pummeled him with her fists.

"Let me go!" she howled. But she was weak from the pot she'd been smoking and that, in combination both with the last draining he'd given her and her current terror of him, had so leeched her of vitality that she could barely make a peep to announce her distress to the night outside.

"Keep quiet, you bitch, or else I'll tear you into little pieces and eat your heart right here and now," he growled at her, baring his fangs at her.

She acquiesced, tears forming in her eyes. "Please, please, baby. Lemme go."

He slapped her back onto the bed. There was no need for her to get dressed so he didn't require her to. Instead, while she wept miserably behind him, River pulled a dark leather jacket on over his shirt. Once he'd strapped Ivy into the desiccating machines in the basement, he'd join the partiers. In fact, he felt it was necessary. Earlier in the night, before he'd come upstairs to look in on Ivy, a svelte redhead had been giving him the eye. He didn't recall her name. Was it Caroline? Anyway, she'd had a lovely neck.

Once satisfied with his appearance, River roughly pulled the still-sobbing woman up off the bed.

"And now, girl, it's time for you to die," he told her as he dragged her through the bedroom door to his private elevator, the one with the button for the building's secret rooms.

"Please, please, don't do this to me!" Ivy sniveled behind him.

He ignored her pleas. At the moment she was finished; incapable of doing anything except bow to his superiority. She was human; he wasn't, and the games were over. Now she was nothing but food.

He punched the elevator controls but the cage didn't arrive. He got out his cellphone and called Pale Joe instead.

"River? What's up, boss?"

"Joe, my fucking elevator's out of commission, and I've a delivery for the drainer."

Joe laughed over the line. "Man, you tired of that Ivy broad already? I thought you enjoyed screwing her."

"She's old news."

"River, you sure are one bloodthirsty sonofabitch. You know that? With bloodsuckers like you around, I sure am glad I ain't human."

"Oh, I just feel like I need some fresh blood." Beside River, Ivy trembled at his words.

Joe laughed. "I'll drink a blood toast to that."

"What's going on with the elevator cage?"

"I dunno. I've been at the party. Look, boss, take the back stairs down. I'll tell Tasha to clear the coast for you. We'll fix the elevator in the morning."

River hung up and dragged Ivy towards the back stairs. She'd stopped weeping now and was trailing along behind him like an animated doll.

Good, he thought coldly as he pushed her ahead of him towards the staircase. *She's finally accepted her place in the pecking order. She's finally understood that she's at the bottom of the food chain.*

He could smell her humanity, smell the delicious blood running through her arteries and veins, the unseen red fluid so sweetly enticing. He felt like biting her neck again.

But, just as River was about to start grinning, another of those horrible nauseating headaches hit him.

He paused, gripping the stairway bannister and waiting for it to pass. Beside him, sensing nothing, his victim waited like a sheep, every hope she'd ever had in her life gone.

The headache and revulsion cleared up. River pushed Ivy ahead of him down the stairs again. The sooner he got killing her out of the way, the better.

CHAPTER 2

VEINS

The party was a good one, with lots of scantily clad hot women and great music, but Mark Benning felt tense as hell. From his table at the rear of the ballroom, he swept his eyes across the room till they met Donny's, then looked farther until he caught Cleo's gaze too. Donny was near the bar, Cleo was dancing with some musclebound guy who'd been trying to get her drunk all night. Mark nodded back at the pair's almost imperceptible nods. It was almost go-time. Their mole in this vampire nightclub had just sent him a phone text informing him that the secret penthouse-to-basement elevator was now out of commission (a simple matter of removing a fuse) and also that River himself was on his way downstairs to the basement.

Mark's thoughts paused as two bikini-clad blondes whirled past him on their way to the ladies' room, both tottering on high heels and with drinks in hand. One of the blondes looked slightly familiar. The other drunken blonde, the one he didn't recognize, blew him a wet kiss as she staggered past; her red lips portals of invitation to pleasure.

Watching her wiggling ass as she sauntered past, Mark didn't even get a hard-on. Ordinarily he'd be all over her. But tonight was for business. Distractions like the pair of departing drunk beauties were the sort of thing that got a guy buried in the ground. Tonight Mark and his fellow VEINS members were here for vampire business.

VEINS stood for Vampire Engagement, Investigation and Neutralization Syndicate.

Damn right, Mark thought. *Tonight were gonna neutralize this frigging place.*

Douglas River was the target. That damn evil bloodsucker had used up his extended lifespan, and Mark intended to ensure this night was the bastard's last on earth. VEINS also had concrete info that the damn vamps were operating a draining machine in the club basement—for draining living humans that was.

And River was running the operation. Mark almost looked forward to meeting the vampire kingpin. Well no, River wasn't exactly a kingpin, he was more like the vampire governor of WV. Besides, in this case, the location was more important than the target. Making a kill here tonight would have symbolic repercussions. This nightclub was the heart of vampire activities in West Virginia. In Pennsylvania and Ohio too, some VEINS intelligence officers claimed.

So striking the vamps here should scare them a little. Getting rid of River would make the bloodsuckers realize that they weren't anywhere near as invulnerable as they prided themselves on being.

Another set of beauties strode past in front of Mark, these ones returning from the ladies'. He stopped thinking for a minute and stared at them as they joined the dance floor, then jerked alert again as his phone buzzed him.

Target's descending the second floor stairs now, the message read. *Time to intercept.*

Mark smiled to himself. *Time to send River to Hell.*

That settled, he got to his feet. He was a dark, smallish man in his late thirties, one whose slight stature belied how strong he actually was. Like Donny and Cleo he was dressed in deceptively lightweight clothes that in reality concealed weapons. The vamps were smart, everyone entering the Haven nightclub went through a scanner for, amongst other things, silver objects. The VEINS's operatives outfits were designed to black out the scanners so the machines showed they were wearing ordinary clothes.

Now Mark moved very fast. In a few seconds, he was out of the ballroom and was striding fast along a rear corridor. His destination was the staircase at the corridor's end. He looked back once, saw that

Donny and Cleo were right behind them, and turned back towards his destination.

"Shit, man," Cleo was saying as they followed. "Thank goodness it's time. If that guy had felt my ass one more time, I'd likely have cut him open."

River wasn't downstairs yet. But Mark could hear the vampire coming down the stairs. And there would be a woman with him, a woman he wanted to bleed to death. The head bloodsucker wouldn't be going to the basement otherwise.

Right then a man stepped out in front of Mark. Mark recognized him from earlier. He was one of the bouncers, a shaven-headed hulk wearing black jeans and a stretched-to-bursting tee shirt. Earlier, Mark hadn't been able to get the make on him: was the guy a vamp or not?

Now the musclebound guy scowled at them. "Hey, what do you three want back here? You can't come this way. This is a private area."

But Mark had seen the bouncer's fangs, slightly retracted, but both still tinted red as if the man had been bleeding someone when he'd heard their voices approaching.

"You're gonna have to go back the way you came," the bouncer said.

The huge man never saw the flicker of metal in Mark's left hand as the silver knife came up. The next moment he was clutching his neck in horror, trying to howl for help, but no sound was coming out. He *was* a vampire: his spilling blood turned black and his flesh too was already turning black around the wound, this instantaneous tide of decay spreading in a black fester. Mark slashed at him again, digging the silver blade deep into the vampire's belly and slicing sideways. Withering guts spilled out of the man.

With a quick step, Mark stepped past the dying vampire. A horrible stink was coming from the creature now and he was scared that their target River might smell it and turn back. He hurried towards the stairway ahead.

Behind him Donny kicked the fast-disintegrating bouncer back into the room he'd stepped out of and shut the door behind him.

At the end of the corridor, a naked woman now stepped down from the bottom step. She looked towards the VEINS operatives, her eyes blank as a heroin addict's, as empty as a terminal vampire victim's would be.

"Help me," she gasped miserably. "Help me, I don't deserve this!"

Then she was shoved violently forward and hit the wall opposite the stairway entrance. The impact stunned her and she slid down the wall to sit motionless on the floor.

By then, however, Mark and his companions had already forgotten about her. Because by then River had stepped down from the stairs and seen them.

"Get him!" Mark yelled. "Don't let him get away!"

But suddenly, almost as if the bouncer had hit an alarm bell before dying, several more vampires entered the corridor.

"You hold them off!" Mark told Donny and Cleo. "I'll take care of River!"

River laughed at that comment. "Yes, come and get me, you pathetic piece of human shit!"

Already he was transforming into a bat-shaped monster.

Mark laughed at River. "Is that the best you can manage, asshole?"

The bat-thing River became was very ugly. Mark had seen several in his time fighting the vampires. Standing upright, the creature was roughly human shaped and about the same size as River had been. It was dark gray in color and had leathery skin with black patches of bristly hair, thin limbs with wing membranes stretched between wrist and ankle on each side, and sharp claws on both hands and feet. The waist was very thin, but the chest very wide. The head was a bat's, very large in proportion to its body—twice as big as it should have been on a human—and the neck very thick, widening in two muscular ridges down to its shoulders. It had massive ears, small red piggish eyes, and a fat snout beneath which long yellow fangs gleamed in the large mouth.

Staring at it, Mark felt the same terror as always. *I must be crazy to keep doing this shit.* The thing smelt as horrible as it looked; the reek of musty old graves.

But someone had to keep the vampires in line, and that's why VEINS existed.

If the transformed vampire was a terrifying sight, in its winged state it was also less able to maneuver in the cramped corridor space. Already it was leaping at Mark and slashing its wings at the intrepid vampire hunter, with its jaws agape to bite him and suck him empty of blood.

Mark followed standard procedure when fighting in cramped spaces like this: don't let yourself get surrounded; always keep an exit behind you. True, it was currently night and the vampires could follow them outside, but it was better to have an option of directions to flee in. And their car was outside as well.

So Mark ducked and rolled under the slashing bat-monster, moving towards the end of the corridor. The vampire flew over him, its heels brushing his brown hair.

Mark leapt back up to his feet and spun around. Slowed by the cramped structure of the corridor, the transformed River was clumsily doing the same. Mark used this short interlude in their combat to do several things:

First, he quickly checked on the others. Cleo had followed his lead, rolling back toward the corridor entrance. Staring around River's huge wings, Mark watched her leap safely to her feet and pull two silver knives from her jacket as she spun to face the vampires.

Donny, however, hadn't been as fortunate as she. One of the three vampires who'd come to River's aid—this one now in wolf form—had clamped its powerful jaws on Donny's right shoulder. Donny squealed in agony as the wolf ripped off his left arm. But even dying, he took the vampire along with him. Consumed by bloodlust, the creature never noticed the short sword Donny swung at it with his right hand. Pure silver met and penetrated wolf flesh. Not deeply, but enough. The wolf howled like mad and began crumpling to ash where it stood. Donny collapsed on top of it.

Mark winced at the creature's noise but knew there was no chance of its death screams being heard out in the club. The music out there was much too loud.

One vamp down, three to go. Unlike the dead wolf, both remaining backup vampires had assumed bat form.

Meanwhile, Cleo had just sprayed a vampire with silver mist. The mist wouldn't kill it, but would blind it if she'd sprayed it in the face. River was completely turned and facing Mark now, so he couldn't see if she'd done this, but he heard the vampire howl its pain.

The monster's pain seemed to startle River too. The vampires couldn't/didn't speak while in monster shape, but the bat-thing tensed suddenly just as it was about to lunge at Mark.

Mark took this additional short pause to pull River's intended blond victim to her feet and shove her behind him towards the back door.

"Go, go!" he urged the naked blonde, who was staring at the monsters in the corridor in stoned disbelief. "Wait in the blue Yukon by the side door. The key's in the glove compartment. If we ain't out in five, drive the hell away from here!"

Mark didn't wait for her reply; couldn't check either if she was complying with his instructions. River was lunging at him again, rage in his red eyes as if incensed at being thwarted of his juicy prey.

Mark still had his silver knife in hand and he rushed to meet the monster. The vampire clearly had the strength advantage, but Mark was trained in close-quarters fighting. The trick was to avoid the fangs and teeth and get in a few good strikes; from a hundred percent silver blade those would prove fatal to the vampire.

They met, with River getting the better of that first exchange. Mark leaned against the wall grimacing from several deep slashes the vampire's claws had torn in his shoulder. Nothing life threatening, but the blood seeping from his wounds only seemed to have further roused his opponent's bloodlust.

For his own part, he was certain he'd slashed the vampire's wing with his knife. Yes, he could see the wound, a jagged tear by River's left hip. But, maybe not—the wound wasn't flaking like a silver wound should.

A quick glance to his left showed him the back door swinging in the night breeze. Clearly, the blonde had taken his advice and made tracks for their SUV.

The monster lunged at him again. Knife held in front of him to ward it off, Mark ducked to his right. This move took him back into the middle of the corridor and so enabled him to witness Cleo's last moments. She was down on her back at the far end of the corridor, her legs kicking violently, with the giant vampire bat she'd misted with silver spray on top of her, its fangs apparently buried in her neck and sucking her dry.

That vampire hadn't won either though. Gusts of ash were already drifting up into the air from its head. And then, suddenly, the giant bat screamed in pain. In twin bursts of stinky black and gray gas, both of Cleo's silver blades erupted from its back as she stabbed it through the belly. The vampire went limp after that and lay on Cleo. Cleo's legs stopped kicking then.

Two vamps left; and Cleo seemed to have injured the other one too; it was leaning against the wall, licking its right forearm.

But River was still alive and attaching Mark again.

Let's get this over with. This time Mark didn't avoid the head vampire. They met and stood toe to toe, snarling at each other in complete hatred of what the other represented. The vampire was stronger, but Mark was a trained soldier; hours in the gym had conditioned him to exquisite perfection. He held River's saliva-dripping snout at bay; River in turn, held Mark's silver blade at bay. Mark had several short stakes and a hammer concealed in the legs of his pants, but in close-quarters fighting like this, such weapons were more of a hindrance than a help. So the knife it was then. One sharp stab up into the heart would do. Then the USA could count one bloodsucker less. Mark felt confident of victory in this conflict. Not because he was tougher than his undead opponent, but because once transformed into a bestial state, vampires weren't much better than the animals they became, their human logic packed away into some primal corridor and the bestial instinct given full reign. This meant they were prone to make mistakes. One of which was impatience. Any moment now, River was sure to grow tired of this straining test of strength and retreat for another lunge at Mark.

Mark, however, had made a fatal mistake of his own. He'd forgotten the other vampire, the wounded one leaning against the wall. He only realized his mistake when the vampire bat's razor-like claws tore into his back. In desperate horror he felt the shredding of his skin and flesh and the spilling of his blood.

So instead, it was Mark who quit the test of strength and attacked River. If he was dying, it had to mean something. And he *was* dying. That much was certain; the unseen vampire behind him had now torn the side of his neck open and his blood was gushing out.

Mark calculated that he had maybe two minutes of life left. He let go of River's neck, then using all the strength he could muster, broke River's grip on his wrist. Then, in a lightning-swift move, he swung his knife back and slit the neck of the vampire who'd just killed him, then bringing that same knife forward again, he slashed River down the front of his body, finally shoving the silver blade all the way through the vampire, just like Cleo had done with her own attacker.

"That's it for you, asshole," he gasped at the vampire bat as he sank to his knees, pulled down to the ground by the dead weight of the dissolving vampire corpse behind him, which still had its claws dug into his shoulders. His fall also jerked his blade completely out of River's body.

Mark hit the floor and lay there. No matter how much he tried to stem its flow with his fingers, his blood was spilling away and he was too drained now to stand and attempt an escape. He was going to die here. But so was River.

Yes, River was going to die too tonight. That thought put a smile on Mark Benning's face.

So imagine Mark's surprise when, staring at the vampire bat he'd just dealt a mortal wound, he saw the thing staggering back to its feet and lurching towards him again. That the undead creature wasn't already decaying was strange enough, but what was stranger still to Mark was the fact that its wound—an unhealable silver-inflicted wound—seemed to be healing.

River, meanwhile, was approaching Mark to finish him off. The giant bat collapsed across the dying vampire hunter's body, knocking what little breath his lungs still contained out of him.

"What the fuck is going on?" Mark gasped, before, with a slow flash of dark claws, River tore his throat out. Mark jerked up with the pain and his eyes gaped open, but there was nothing he could do now except die. And die knowing he'd somehow gloriously failed in his mission to exterminate River.

Too weak to move, the vampire lay where it had fallen and drank the blood spurting from Mark's neck. As he faded into death's dark embrace, Mark felt River's satisfaction at having killed him.

River was the only vampire still left in the hall, the other three now having become smoking piles of ash. As its body healed, the wounded vampire bat enjoyed the sweet taste of Mark Benning's death.

CHAPTER 3

Exit Ivy

In the blue GMC Yukon parked by the nightclub's side entrance, Ivy Rain waited ten long minutes for the man who'd saved her and directed her to the vehicle to arrive. Each of those ten minutes felt like her entire lifetime being replayed over and over. The fact that River had earlier leeched her of blood and she felt close to fainting made her wait seem longer and more horrible. The fact that she was naked made the interval all the more surreal.

The Haven club building loomed beside her like Death's shadow. Three floors and a basement filled with pleasure and agony. Three floors and a basement of bliss and destruction.

Finally, it dawned on Ivy that her savior wouldn't be exiting the club after all.

On reaching the Yukon, Ivy had naturally sat in its front passenger seat, but now she moved over to the driver's seat.

Where's the starter key? Oh, in the glove compartment.

A quick fumble in there produced the key. She slotted it in the ignition and turned it. She felt an intense surge of relief when the car instantly started.

After a further minute's wait to ensure that, yes, her rescuer really wasn't going to emerge from the club, Ivy drove off.

She paid little attention to where she was headed. So long as she kept the blue vehicle moving away from that horrible Haven nightclub, she didn't care where she went right now.

Driving away from her private hell, Ivy Rain felt traumatized by everything she'd experienced this night. She doubted that she would ever get over it.

But one thing was for certain: it'd be another lifetime before she ever returned to this damned Mountain State again.

CHAPTER 4

River . . . Friday Morning, 6 a.m.

This morning Douglas River wondered why he was still alive. He lay in his bed with the drapes drawn (and the windows behind them blacked off by special lightproof panels) and pondered his miraculous survival. The lights were off and he lay in perfect darkness.

Hell no, I shouldn't be alive. He stabbed me with a silver knife. Silver is Kryptonite to us vampires, and that stuff felt like it was one hundred percent pure.

River didn't actually know what being stabbed by pure silver felt like, but he'd often imagined the horrible agony of undead flesh penetrated by the metal.

And he had the remains of the other victims—his companions—as his assurance that the metal had had lethal tendencies. Tasha, David, Anton and James were all dead. With a hand he traced the scar on his belly, still painful, but definitely healed.

So, why the hell aren't I dead too?

River tried to sleep but couldn't. This was another thing. For the past two days, his sleeping patterns had been disrupted. Where before he'd lie in bed at sunup and not rouse again until an hour after sundown, for the past two nights, he'd slept beside Ivy like a stone.

I'm sick, he decided. *That must be the explanation of why I'm having trouble sleeping. But what kind of sickness makes a vampire immune to silver?*

He got out of bed in the darkness and walked over to the fridge for a drink of blood. He got out the blood jar and poured himself a glass. Then he sat on his favorite couch and stared at the room. The bedroom had special fluorescent bulbs, but he felt no need for them. His eyes were as attuned to the darkness as a cat's.

He sipped the blood and his thoughts turned to Ivy.

She got away! Her escape angered River. Not the waste of her blood—she wasn't that important; human women were a dime a dozen—but the fact that it marked a security lapse on his own part. Not good at all. She was the first to ever escape from him.

For all I know, she could be reporting me to the police right now.

Then he smiled at his own naivety. *And what will she tell them? That I'm a vampire? Well, yeah, she does have the bite marks to prove that much.* He ran a finger over his teeth, fangs retracted now. *But hey, you hallucinating human bitch, where are my fangs that I bit you with?*

He began laughing at the spectacle of Ivy Rain trying to convince the stolid law enforcement officers that she was telling the truth. They might even believe her at first, until she told them about his fight with the vampire hunters in the corridor and about the vampires' magical transformations into wolves and bats. Then it would be out of the door for Ivy Rain, and she'd be glad if she didn't end up undergoing psychiatric evaluation too.

River forgot about Ivy. She wasn't important, just the one that got away. No one would ever corroborate her tale. None of last night's partiers had suspected the life and death struggle happening just a few steps away from where they were dancing and flirting with each other. Even the girls powdering their faces in the nearby ladies' room hadn't heard the noise of the scuffle.

Of course, if Ivy Rain did insist on becoming a pain in the ass, it should be no difficulty to hunt her down and send her down the basement anyway. Finding Ivy should be easy. Her purse and ID were still here in his bedroom.

But at the moment, River had more important matters that an escapee to occupy him. Things like Max King's arrival tonight.

River sipped some more blood, then put the glass down. *Yeah, I'm ill, for real. Even blood tastes strange to me. Once it's nightfall, I'll drive over to see Dr. Xerxes. Max King won't arrive from Richmond till say eleven-thirty, so if I get to the clinic by nine p.m., I'll have time to spare. Thank Hades the headaches seem to have stopped.*

That was one positive. He'd not thrown up since the fight. But memory of the fight brought fresh worries and anger:

Those VEINS shitheads again. They must've had inside help. When we checked the elevator it was working perfectly . . . but Pale Joe said . . .

For a moment the finger of suspicion formed in his mind and pointed at Pale Joe. Had Joe set him up to be killed so he could take over his position? Apart from River, Joe was the only other club-vamp who'd not been killed last night. He'd said he'd been screwing some human girl at the time and had told Tasha to secure the corridor for River's descent. That made sense, but River didn't trust Joe. No, he didn't trust Pale Joe at all. But what if Joe wasn't the one who'd set him up for VEINS? God knew those human idiots didn't need anyone encouraging them on their misguided cause. They were like soldier ants. You killed a hundred of them and a hundred more instantly took their place.

Dammit! I need to investigate the human staff here. Personally vet everyone Tony employs. And I gotta keep the new vamp staff on high alert all the while Mr. King and his daughter are visiting town. I can't have any nonsense happening while they're here.

River wasn't letting anything or anyone get in the way of his ambitions. He was particularly interested in meeting Alexia King, whom he'd heard was quite beautiful.

Who knew, maybe the pair of them might even hit it off romantically and then . . .

Vampires were predators. Vampire society ran on wheels of respect and fear, not bonds of love. Lions and tigers didn't love each other. Like the big cats, vampires associated from necessity, understanding the concept of strength in numbers; forming alliances with each other mainly to strengthen themselves. Each was a born social climber, ready to stab even their lovers in the back to advance themselves closer to their leaders.

Before he could picture himself and Alexia King at the altar, River yawned. Finally he felt sleep calling to him. And now, he was certain that despite his perplexing illness he'd sleep a normal, uninterrupted vampire sleep.

He drained the glass of blood, though the blood made him feel somewhat queasy, then retired to bed again. Before lying down he called the BSS clinic and made a doctor's appointment for that evening.

This time he managed to fall asleep. He dreamt of biting virgin necks and draining their young and trembling bodies.

CHAPTER 5

River . . . Friday Evening

At a quarter past seven that evening, Douglas River began dressing for his doctor's appointment.

He'd woken up at six and had already had his bath. He felt very refreshed. The scar on his belly had already erased itself; its pain was all gone.

Except that he knew the weapon should have killed him. *But it somehow didn't and I intend to find out why.*

River had woken to a WhatsApp message informing him Max King would be arriving on schedule at 10:30, riding into Morgantown in a black stretch limousine. Most of the state's top vampires would coming to the nightclub to welcome him.

Three new vampire staff had already arrived and taken over the jobs of those who'd died last night.

Considering the importance of tonight's ceremony, and the amount of preparations yet to be finalized, River had considered whether or not he should cancel his doctor's appointment, but in the end he had decided against doing so. Blood still tasted bitter on his tongue and he didn't want to wind up puking over Mr. King's clothes at some point during the night's revels. What a hell of a way *to not* impress the old man that would be.

No more headaches either, so maybe nothing's actually wrong with me, just overwork or too much sex with Ivy and . . .

It was then that River realized that something was *very* wrong with him. In fact that anomaly had been literally staring him in the face for the twenty minutes that he'd been getting dressed.

Douglas River hadn't seen his reflection in over a hundred years. Neither in a mirror, nor in water either. Vampires didn't cast reflections; even their clothes didn't show up in mirrors. Nor did they appear in photos.

In fact, the only reason River had a mirror in his penthouse suite at all was because of his many girlfriends. The ladies all got upset if they couldn't see how pretty they'd made themselves.

And this was the reason why River at first overlooked the image in the luxury dresser's mirror. It wasn't until he was pulling on his shoes that he realized he could see himself reflected on its silvered glass.

He couldn't see himself clearly. No, his reflection actually looked like a fading ghost in there—it was little more than a faint colored-in outline, plus he could see all of the bedroom furniture through himself. But to a century-plus-old man who hardly remembered what he looked like anymore, even that faintest of images was a shock.

There was no doubt about it. There was a vampire in the mirror now, and the vampire was himself.

Suddenly River felt very, very afraid. *Oh shit. Yeah, I've gotta see the doc and quick at that.*

He hurried through lacing his shoes, grabbed his car keys and dashed out the bedroom door.

Once in the corridor that led to the stairs, however, River put a determined effort into calming himself. No matter what, he needed to project an atmosphere of normalcy to the club staff he would shortly encounter downstairs. To do this, he tried to focus on the club itself, this vampire edifice he supervised, this large building in the northeast of Morgantown.

Though the Haven nightclub's three-story building wasn't a hotel, its third floor was exclusively residential. In addition to River's own quarters, the building's top floor contained three other first-class suites reserved solely for visiting vampire dignitaries.

River stepped down onto the second floor landing. Looking down the long second floor corridor, he saw Olivia Riley, the club accountant, entering her office. This floor was mainly offices, but also housed some of the club's vampire staff.

Downstairs on the first floor, the club was gearing up for the night's revelry. This ground floor was where all the action was. Most of the Haven's patrons—both human *and* vampire—never even climbed the stairs to the second floor.

River peeked into the ballroom and nodded. Tony Petrelli, the Haven club's human 'day manager' already had the tables and the "WELCOME TO WV, MAX KING!" banner set up.

He waved to Tony, then ducked his head out of there before the man could ask him any questions.

"Hey, River . . ." Pale Joe said behind him. "How are we gonna—?"

River quickly turned around and cut Joe off. He was in too much of a hurry.

"Later," he insisted harshly, then hurried for the front entrance.

CHAPTER 6

Dr. Xerxes & the Vampire Elite

Arnold Xerxes was one of the USA's foremost vampire associates (or collaborators, as VEINS coldly termed them).

***

There were less than ten thousand vampires in the USA, which came to about two hundred in each of the fifty states. There could have been a lot more, of course, seeing as all that was required to turn someone was either to drink them to death or feed them vampire blood, but the vampires, conscious of the crucial need to remain anonymous, kept a firm rein on their own numbers. Only the very rich amongst their victims were ever permitted to join the exalted vampire ranks. The rest were beheaded outright. But of course, there were a few that got away, and who later had to be accepted into the ranks. No system is ever perfect.

The unseen society of vampires kept their tenuous grip on power by means of their collaborators. These were humans sworn to silence during hideous and obscene vampire rituals and promised future vampirism using unbreakable vampire oaths. (Any vampires who dared kill a collaborator were themselves killed and their drained blood used to turn the next set of inductees.)

Collaborators were thus honorary vampires and knew all of the group's secrets. Able to walk in daylight, they ran everything for the vampire society until they were sixty years old, when in a ceremony to welcome them permanently into the undead darkness, they drank vampire blood and became vampires themselves. At this ceremony, the new vampires also partook of an elixir that restored some of their youth. At this point, one could choose one's target age, on the understanding that once set, it would remain permanent.

Exceptions to the age-of-entrance rule were made in cases where a candidate suffered an almost fatal accident or contracted an extremely debilitating illness.

***

Dr. Arnold Xerxes was also one of the planet's few experts on undead diseases.

With lavish vampire funding, Xerxes had set up Blood Specialist Services, Inc. (BSS for short). The clinic's stated aim and goal was to "Spearhead research into the eradication of blood diseases." To this end, the BSS complex on Ventura Drive also housed one of West Virginia's largest and best-equipped blood banks.

It was a genius front, of course—the blood bank provided the state's vampires with all the blood they needed; while at the same time the BSS clinic also served as their own private hospital, though there were occasional questions asked as to why most of the clinic's patients only visited or were discharged after dark.

In his current position Dr. Arnold Xerxes was above suspicion in the human world.

In his own way, though still too young to be turned, the man was vampire elite.

CHAPTER 7

River & Dr. Xerxes

"This is extremely troubling," Dr. Xerxes said, making a steeple of his fingers on the edge of his desk.

"I dare say it is," River agreed. "It's the craziest thing—I'm suddenly immune to silver and I can see myself in the mirror again."

"Judging from what you told me, your immunity to silver saved your life last night."

"Yeah, it did. But now that really bothers me."

The doctor was about River's supposed age of thirty-five. He was handsome and tall and women liked him. Men respected him. Even River, who was now so distant in time from being human that he naturally looked down on them, accepted that Arnold Xerxes was a man to be respected.

Dr. Xerxes got his feet, then pointed to the bed behind River's chair. "Well, let's have a look at you."

River got up, removed his shirt, and lay on the bed. The next few minutes were taken up by the doctor's probing.

"Open your mouth and stick out your fangs."

River did so. Despite the situation, he found this medical exam somewhat amusing. With his heightened vampire senses, he could hear the pulsing of blood through Xerxes's arteries, especially when the man leaned in close. The joke in this was in controlling his natural instinct to bite the doctor in the neck. Of course, he didn't. Xerxes wouldn't find that funny in the least.

"Good. Now protract and retract them several times. Yes, like that. No problems there, and the holes look normal and unblocked. And you've lost the taste for blood?"

"Not *lost* it, doc. It just doesn't taste as sweet anymore."

"And your desire for blood? Is that still normal, River?"

"I still feel it, but sometimes I feel disgusted at myself for feeling it and . . ."

More prodding and probing. Dr. Xerxes placing a stethoscope on River's chest. "But always after the headaches? This disgust, I mean. It only occurs after the headaches?"

"Yeah, yeah, only after the headaches. But those seem to have stopped. I haven't had a headache today."

River answered Xerxes's questions with only half of his mind; the other half was reviewing his preparations for the night's entertainment. Which reminded him to question Xerxes: "Doc, did either Joe or Tony forward my request for virgin's blood to you?"

Dr. Xerxes grinned down at him. "For Mr. King's cocktails? Yeah, they did."

"Did you have any on hand? I know it's a hard order to fill, but . . ."

"Maybe, but I'm not sure."

"Not sure, how?"

Dr. Xerxes laughed. "Best solution Mildred came up with was what I'd call 'religious teens' blood.

"Huh?" Mildred was the doctor's secretary.

"You know—the girls from the Catholic school down the road. During our last blood drive, they participated en-masse for a good cause. I'm assuming those young ladies are all saving themselves for marriage, so . . ."

River nodded. "That'll have to do."

Dr. Xerxes took a blood sample from him. The prick of the shiny needle reminded River of that other stabbing that for some reason hadn't killed him.

"Alright, you can sit up now," the doctor said afterwards. "But don't put your shirt on yet. I've one last test."

River sat up and waited, his left thumb pressing the wad of cotton the doctor had placed in the crook of his elbow to stop the bleeding.

The doctor, meanwhile, had moved to his office door and opened it.

"Mildred, please bring me a mirror. Any at all."

"Yes, doctor. What size?"

"Not too big."

The doctor shut the office door and returned to his vampire patient. "I want to see this reflection of yours for myself," he explained.

River nodded. "Are you attending the reception tonight."

Xerxes shook his head. "Too much damn work to get through."

"You should try to make it, doc. Should be quite a party. When last did you have some fun?"

"I can't remember, seems like when I was still in diapers. But I really can't get away tonight. Someone brought in a boy with leukemia and he's in a bad way. How long is the old guy in town for anyway?"

"Just a week, then he's off to Chicago."

Mildred Wilson entered then with a two-feet by one-foot mirror. The doctor's secretary was a serious-looking woman in her mid-forties who was also a vampire associate. On the doctor's instructions, she stood the mirror upright on the foot of the bed River was sitting on, then, keeping it in place with one hand, stood to one side of it so she too could see what her boss was looking at.

River was once again treated to the spectacle of viewing his ghostly self. Now, his reflection seemed a little sharper. Nowhere near as solid or well-defined as either Xerxes's or Mildred's did, but River felt his reflection definitely appeared more opaque.

"Yeah, it's just like you described," Xerxes said after a few moments of close scrutiny. "Alright, Mildred, you can take it away." As she picked it up, he added, "Did Jerry say when he'll be coming to fix the office intercom?"

She shook her head. "He's still in the building though; so maybe before I leave for home."

"Please call him and remind him. I can't keep walking to the office door each time I need you for something."

Mildred departed with the mirror. River pulled his shirt and jacket back on. Then he crossed the large room and once more sat opposite Xerxes.

"So, what do you think?" he asked the other man. He felt unaccountably strange. Though Xerxes had kept up a smooth flow of friendly, if professional chatter throughout his examination of River, the vampire sensed a disturbance in the man. Just like when he'd first detailed his symptoms, the doctor once more seemed very unsettled, though he was clearly doing his best to conceal his worries from his patient.

"C'mon, doc, don't keep me in suspense," River joked. "I ain't dying, am I?"

Dr. Xerxes shook his head. "No, not at all. In a sense it would be more accurate to say that you're *living*."

"Huh? Doc, that don't make any sense. Am I evolving into a higher, super type of vampire?"

The doctor sighed. "No, River, I think you're becoming human again."

The vampire gaped at the doctor. "What?" Then, after a pause during which he tried to digest the news and failed, he asked, "Doc, how is that even possible?"

Dr. Xerxes leaned back in his chair and rolled it back from his desk. "I must assume that during your long period undead, you'll have heard of a condition called *humanitis*?"

Humanitis? River thought on that. "Yeah, I've heard about it—a mythical vampire disease caught from humans, which . . ." He gaped at the doctor again. "You're saying I've caught *that*? That I've got humanitis?"

"Hmm, well I won't be sure until I get your blood tested and examine your blood cells under a microscope, but the symptoms all fit."

"But, man, it's a mythological illness! A fairy tale."

Dr. Xerxes shook his head, his face set in grim lines. "Not a fairy tale. Just something hardly worth bothering about. Humanitis is so extremely rare that . . . well, view it this way: a vampire has a one in two hundred million chance of catching it. Less chance than winning the Powerball lottery. Who'd ever worry about something like that?"

River nodded. "And you think *I've* caught it?"

"I'll be honest with you—yes."

River still found the information difficult to process. "So what now? No . . . first of all: If I've got humanitis, how did I catch it?"

"From a human, of course."

"Yeah, but how?"

"I'm not sure. Maybe sex, maybe not—the myths aren't clear. You got any human girlfriends at the moment?"

"One; she left last night." River felt too perplexed to explain to Xerxes the detailed circumstances of Ivy's escape.

The doctor shook his head as if Ivy's departure explained everything. But River didn't think so. He honestly doubted that his life could be altered so completely by a chance encounter with a human woman. "Fill me in on what I've got," he said. "Is there a cure for this humanitis?"

The doctor frowned. "Well, this isn't Transylvania in the Dark Ages. This is the modern world, where modern medical techniques work miracle cures. So, I suppose that, yes, given time we can cure you." Then he laughed. "Lighten up, at the very worst, you'll become completely human and then simply undergo another vampire induction."

River pondered that. "That ain't too bad." He smiled. "So . . . I'll just keep picking up more and more human traits?"

"And losing your vampire ones," Dr. Xerxes added. "You'll keep getting more human and less vampire."

"How long will all this take?"

"I don't know. Maybe a month, maybe six. The primary way you'll be able to tell how far the conversion's gone is by the state of your reflection. The more solid it becomes—the more opaque—the more human you are. I couldn't detect a heartbeat yet, but in about a week or so, you should have one."

The idea that his heart might actually start beating again intrigued Douglas River.

"So, what do I do now?" he questioned the doctor.

"Well, the first thing you need to do is keep quiet about your condition. The one thing we don't need now is a mob of panicking vamps. There's lots of hag-bloodsucker tales out there about how contagious and dangerous humanitis is. So don't say anything about this to any of the other vampires."

This comment reminded River of the doctor's unease. Even now, while speaking reassuringly, the man still seemed worried about something.

"What're you worried about, doc?" River asked.

"That someone might kill you before we cure you."

"Huh? But I survived the stabbing last night."

"A freak occurrence. Your returning humanity prevented the silver weapon from disintegrating you, and also forced your body to heal the mortal wound. But don't expect it to happen again. And from now on, remember that just about any human weapon might kill you. So don't get shot by any angry girlfriends."

River gulped. Yes, that was definitely something to worry about.

CHAPTER 8

Dr. Xerxes

Once River left his office, Dr. Xerxes sat motionless in his chair for a few minutes. His thoughts were grim, intensely black.

Oh, it had to happen. A one-in-ten-million chance and it just had to happen.

Arnold Xerxes was very committed to the vampire cause. He intended to become a vampire someday and live forever. Both of Xerxes's parents had died while he was in his twenties—his mother of lung cancer and his father in a car crash—and since then he'd been obsessed with the idea of extending his lifespan. When the vampires had approached him with their proposal that he join them, he'd leapt at the opportunity. Since then he'd not regretted his decision for a day. Eternal life wasn't a thing to be sniffed at.

But now, it looked like his dream of eternal life was about to go up in smoke.

After a quarter hour of moody, unpleasant thoughts, he picked up his cellphone and dialed a number.

After a few rings, a cool upper-crust female voice replied: "Arnie, darling, how lovely to hear from you! Are you coming to Max's welcoming party? It's certain to be a blast."

"No, Mina, I've too much work to get through tonight. Listen, Mina, we've a big problem."

The gaiety slowly drained from her voice. "A problem? Now? Can't it wait? I'm trying to get drunk here. Oh, I adore Max, but he's such a bore at times; has no idea of how to have a good time. He's certain to make a long 'Thank You' speech, and also to tell us all about the importance of our vampy heritage and how we the undead are Evil's chosen few. Not that I dispute such claims, but all I'm interested in doing tonight is getting drunk and shaking my ass to some catchy tunes."

"No, Mina, this can't wait. It concerns that vampire heritage you just mentioned. If we don't work fast, it might not exist for much longer."

"Arnie, what are you talking about?"

"It's River. He's caught humanitis. He's becoming human."

"What?" Xerxes could visualize the transformation in Mina Cupples over the phone, the woman's gray eyes widening, her whiskey-and-blood cocktail falling from her fingers and spilling onto the carpet. When next she spoke, her voice bore not the slightest trace of merriment. "He's *what?* Are you sure?"

"Yes, I'm sure. The man just left my office. There's nothing to panic about yet. The disease is still in its early stages. But . . ."

"I'll be right over. Where are you? The office?"

"Yes."

"I'll be there in twenty minutes. Looks like my long-anticipated partying's just been cancelled."

"Bring Nick with you."

"He's right here with me, wondering what I'm getting so flustered about."

"Alright, I'll see you two shortly."

Dr. Xerxes hung up. Then he got up from his desk and walked over to stare out of his office window; down at the clinic's front parking lot.

A few moments later there was a tap on his office door.

"Yes?"

Mildred poked her head in. "Jerry's here to fix the intercom, doctor," she said. "Should I send him on in?"

Xerxes sighed with relief. Then he remembered his meeting with the vampires in twenty minutes. Maybe insufficient time for the clinic's communications technician to work out why his office intercom had packed up; and Jerry Foley wasn't a vampire associate.

"No, ask him to come back tomorrow morning," he whispered to Mildred. "We're about to have a vampy conference. And when he's gone, get your recording equipment and come sit in with us."

She nodded and ducked out of the door again. After spending some more time staring out at the parking lot, a very troubled Arnold Xerxes returned to his desk to await his undead visitors.

CHAPTER 9

Crystal

Crystal Barkley was on her fifth run of carrying wine glasses from the Haven club's kitchen to its ballroom when her cellphone buzzed with a text message notification.

Crystal, a short young woman with dirty-blonde hair, had been feeling on edge all day. This, combined with this unexpected buzzing of her phone, made her drop her tray of glasses. The thick corridor rug prevented a complete disaster, but she lost four glasses to cracked stems.

That's coming outa my paycheck.

Kneeling over the fallen tableware, Crystal got out her cellphone and checked the message that had startled her. It was from Josie; short and succinct and alarming:

Crys, get ur ass home rt nw. This is a fn emergency.

The message's tone instantly filled Crystal with dread. She was still on edge after the previous night's failed assassination attempt. This just made her anticipations worse.

Had the vampires discovered their involvement in the plot to kill River? Crystal didn't see how that was possible, but it could have happened. She'd been ultra-careful when slipping into the basement to remove the fuse from the vampire's secret elevator. No one had been in the area at the time. The same level of caution had gone into her replacing the fuse.

Also, to make doubly certain that Crystal wouldn't be noticed, both times that she'd visited the basement, Josie had been in the CCTV surveillance room, giving blowjobs to Pete the Security Guy.

They'd flipped a coin for it and Josie had lost. She got the blowjobs, Crystal got the fuse job. Josie had bitched about that: "Alright, but I'm only sucking his dick. I ain't fucking him."

"Whatever. I don't care if you only give him a hand job. Just make certain he ain't watching the monitors for fifteen minutes. If I get caught . . ."

But it had come off alright. And afterwards when they'd met up again, Josie had pointedly refused to state what she'd done with Pete each time. Pete, though, had been smiling contentedly all through today. So maybe Josie had fucked him after all.

But now? Crystal regarded the text again: *This is a fn emergency? Shit, what's happened now?*

She sent Josie a quick reply: *Be rt over!*

'Home' was right next door. VEINS had made certain that Crystal and Josie would be sleeping right beside the enemy. All Crystal needed to do was slip out of the back door and sneak across the car park. But first she needed to clean up the mess.

Yeah, a mess, just like last night's fiasco. Three VEINS operatives dead and we didn't get River. Then she smiled a little. *But there's four vampires missing from work today and four new vampire employees. So the attack wasn't a total loss.*

She hurried down to the broom closet and returned with a broom and a dustpan. She quickly swept up the shards of glass and disposed of them. Then, seeing as her previous burden of tableware had ended up on the floor, she took the unbroken wine glasses back to the kitchen for washing. This time Ron the chief waiter gave her a cart of clean tableware to deliver to the ballroom—plates, glasses, cutlery. Glaringly absent amongst the cutlery were any silver utensils, confirming that tonight's party was a vampire one.

The thought of the bloodsucker's feast filled Crystal with an anger which was greater than her fear of discovery.

She delivered the cart to the ballroom. She wasn't allowed inside the hall, further confirmation of the exclusive nature of tonight's revelry. Annabelle Robinson, a pale middle-aged woman who'd been employed at the nightclub just this morning as Tasha's replacement, accepted the cart from Crystal and wheeled it away out of sight. Crystal smiled politely at the new junior manager. Of course, the woman was a vampire. There was no way of telling for certain though, except by either using a thermometer or by staking her. And she had the obligatory swollen vampire lips, like she'd had lip enhancement injections.

Before the ballroom door shut behind Annabelle, Crystal once more caught a glimpse of the bright red banner the vampires had spread across the far wall of the ballroom: "WELCOME TO WV, MAX KING!"

Who the hell is Max King? Crystal wondered as she turned and headed back down the corridor to the kitchen. Now the urgency of the cellphone message burned in her mind.

"Hey, Crys, we aren't finished yet. Where are you going?"

She'd been just about to slip out of the side door when the day manager's voice stopped her.

Shit!

She turned to face him, a pained smile on her face. Tony Petrelli was a large man; strict at times, but nice enough. But then he was also a vampire collaborator. Anyone who'd make an alliance with those bloodsuckers was merely playing nice. Crystal hoped she'd be alive when the vamps turned him, so she could stake him herself. (For obvious reasons, the Haven club needed a human daytime manager as well as a vampire nighttime one.)

"Sorry, Mr. Petrelli, but my period just started. I'm hurrying next door to slip in a tampon. I'll be right back."

"Uh, yeah," he said disconcerted by the feminine lie. She knew most men had no idea how to react when a women mentioned she was having her monthly red visitor. "Yeah, yeah, but hurry it up. We'll try to make do without you for a while."

Crystal slipped out into the night. She was relieved. She'd been lucky that no vampire had been close while she'd been lying to Tony. Vampires could smell blood on you. They'd have known right away that she was lying. When she was coming back, she'd remember to bring a pack of tampons with her, and show it to at least one of the other waitresses.

Crystal dashed between the border of trees that separated the nightclub from its neighbor building. (Morgantown had lots of woods and surrounding mountains, and large lengths of Easton Mill Road was just forest.) Then she slipped in the back door of she and Josie's small bungalow and hurried through to the living room. Josie was sitting opposite the TV, with the sound turned low. She had a coke by her side and her laptop in her lap. She didn't seem worried; instead she appeared very excited. Crystal hoped Josie wasn't high again. Her nerves were in no condition to handle such nonsense.

"What's the problem?" she asked. "Are they onto us?"

Josie shook her head. Josie Ottman was the same age as Crystal—twenty-six—but taller. Unlike Crystal, whose long blonde hair was held back in a ponytail by a clip, Josie's brown locks were trimmed boyishly short.

"Nah, the vamps don't suspect a damn thing about our involvement in last night's nasty business."

Crystal's relief was mingled with frustration. "So, what's so important then, that you had to set my heart running at triple pace and bring me all the way home? Why couldn't you simply wait till my shift ends?" Josie also worked at Haven, but today she'd done the morning shift. For a moment, Crystal was struck by the nature and the peril of their job. As far as she could tell, none of Haven's other human employees believed that the undead actually existed outside of Bram Stoker, Anne Rice, and Hollywood, talk less of suspecting the undead of being their employers.

"The bug in Xerxes's office just burped out a transmission."

"So? It does that all the time. Most of it's run-of-the mill crap. I, for one, don't want to listen to another recording of some vamp slut describing her herpes symptoms."

"You'll wanna hear this one."

"What's so special about it?"

Josie grinned. "Well, apparently, River—our boss—has picked up some medical condition that's turning him human again. That's why he's still alive after last night's attack."

Crystal was already hurrying over to sit beside Josie. "Play it, play it!"

This sounded like gold.

Crystal wasn't technically inclined, so she waited impatiently while Josie located the file and adjusted its playback volume. Josie finally handed her a spare pair of headphones and they both listened to the audio recording again, with Crystal gaping at the other young woman every minute or so. She was aware that she was expected back at the nightclub, but she could explain away a fifteen minute delay as crippling period pains. And besides, she was certain Mr. Petrelli would be too busy with his last minute party preparations to remember her anyway.

"What the hell!!?" she exclaimed to Josie afterwards. "This is just insane."

"Yeah, I can hardly believe that there's such a thing as *humanitis* and that River's caught it." She frowned. "Ugh, even the name of the disease—makes us humans sound like an inferior species or something."

Crystal frowned. "To the vamps *we are* an inferior species. They think of us as food. They neither love nor hate us; except when we're hunting and killing them, they consider us too unimportant to bother about." She got to her feet. "Well, later, housie, I gotta go."

Josie raised a finger. "Wait. There's a second file to listen to."

Crystal shook her head. "I can't stay. Just summarize it, I can hear the entire thing when I get back later."

"Well, apparently, Xerxes lied to River. What he's got's really bad. The vampires are gonna have a conference about it in about five minutes."

"Just keep recording it. And also try to find out who the hell Max King is."

"Who's that?"

"The guy the vamps are giving tonight's party for."

Crystal left Josie and hurried into the bathroom. She got a new pack of tampons out from the medicine cabinet and ran back outside.

"See you later!" she called to Josie, then shut the door and hurried back to work. As she let herself back in through the side door, her mind was filled with a strange exhilaration. If things were as serious as Josie had mentioned, then the vampires just might be in the middle of a crisis.

Crystal couldn't help but smile at that. She hated the vampires with a deep passion and as far as she was concerned, the more trouble they got into, the better.

CHAPTER 10

The Conference

With a forbidding loud beating of massive wings, the two vampires arrived on the roof of the BSS clinic. The night was dark, with a threat of rain; the vampires could have been parts of thunderclouds that had fragmented and fallen to earth. Watching the dark creatures descend from the sky, Arnold Xerxes felt a scintillating awe threaten to overpower him. Yes, this was what he wanted—this dark power that despite its diurnal limitations terrified the average man. True, the vampire was an evil species, but it was a beautiful evil; an evil that had survived the grave. Triumph over death was beautiful in itself and something to be desired.

Pondering how it was that a vampire's animal alterations affected their clothes also, Arnold Xerxes waited patiently while the arriving duo transformed back to human form. Then, after kissing the woman on both cheeks and shaking hands with her male companion, he led the vampires to the rooftop elevator designed specifically for such aerial arrivals.

He was silent till they arrived in his office.

Xerxes courteously seated the pair at his office desk then took his seat opposite them. While waiting for them to speak, he studied the two vampires.

Mina Cupples looked fifty and had black hair and gray eyes. In reality she was about two hundred years old and was currently using up her seventh identity—her last name had been Amy Forrest. Switching identities was a permanent problem when one lived forever. You either masqueraded as your own offspring (this worked best for vampires who looked to be in their twenties or thirties), or you became a different person every thirty or so years. The latter option involved a lot of paperwork, but the vampire society had sufficient money and influence in the US government to make it happen smoothly.

So, in ten- or fifteen-years' time Mina Cupples would become maybe Mary Harris, or Jane Coulter, or . . . the possibilities seemed endless.

Xerxes felt a shiver of horror. But all that might change soon, if Douglas River . . .

He smiled at Mina. She was an attractive woman, if a little stout as a result of all the drinking she did. But then, he assumed that if the only life one ever knew was nightlife, there was little chance of one not picking up some sort of a drinking habit. Vampires gained weight slower than humans—blood had very few calories in it—but they could add on the pounds if they tried. And alcohol was great for accomplishing that.

Mina was still dressed for tonight's party, in a low-cut green evening dress. Her boyfriend Nick Anderson was similarly formally dressed in a brown tuxedo.

Nick was a hundred years old, but looked forty. As a human being he'd been a soldier. He had actually fought at the Dunkirk evacuation during WW2. Of middle height and quite muscular, tonight the dark-haired man also looked very worried.

If Douglas River fit the profile of state governor, Mina Cupples and Nick Anderson were in charge of handling West Virginia's vampire security.

Nick was the one who opened their conversation:

"I thought humanitis was just a bar joke. And you're saying it actually exists?"

Two name changes ago, Mina Cupples had studied medicine. "I've been telling him this isn't some kind of a joke," she told Xerxes, "but he still thinks we're pulling his leg. Maybe *you'll* have more luck convincing him."

Xerxes nodded and stared evenly at Nick. His secretary Mildred sat off to one side, taking notes and also recording everything onto a digital voice recorder.

"She's right," he assured Nick. "River *is* a carrier of the dreaded humanitis."

Nick settled back into his seat to ponder on this. Xerxes turned his attention to Mina.

"Does River suspect anything about its severity yet?" she asked him.

"Nothing. I told him it's curable."

"But it isn't, is it?"

"No, he's going to keep degenerating back to the human norm. There's no fix."

Mina nodded solemnly. "How long before he becomes infectious?"

"Two weeks at the outside. After which any contact between River and a vampire will spread the disease."

"Fill me in on the details of this humanitis," Nick said. "From the way you and Mina look, it involves way more than just becoming alive again, doesn't it?"

Xerxes nodded. "A whole lot more. What the ancient texts say— and what River doesn't know—is that after he becomes human, the disease will begin to consume his humanity."

Nick looked to Mina for confirmation of this.

"Yes it will," she agreed. "The disease will eat away his mind and when that's gone it will start on his body, till in the end all that's left of the once proud and beautiful vampire is a slug. A giant, slimy, mindless gastropod the shape and color of dog poop."

"Shit," Nick said, his face worried. "Shit."

Mina shuddered. "Now I need a drink. Blood with a dash of whiskey in it."

"One for me too," Nick said, his face pale.

Xerxes looked at Mildred, who nodded back, then set down her pad and exited the office. "I'll fetch the whole bottle," she said. "I need a drink too."

Xerxes fell silent now. He'd given the vampires the information he had. It was left for them to determine what course of action to take. He was still human after all, and had to defer to their decisions even if he disagreed with their intended course of action. And besides, this was a matter of security, not of medicine.

Nick rose from his chair and began pacing the office. "There's really only one course of action open to us," he said. "We must neutralize River before he becomes a threat to the entire vampire race. I hate to do this, 'cos I like the guy, but we have to capture him and kill him."

He leaned on the doctor's desk and stared at Mina. "Do you agree, darling?"

She nodded. "One man's life is nothing compared to that of everyone else. So, yes, we eradicate River to save the vampire race."

Mildred came in then with mixed drinks for everyone. In addition, as promised, she'd brought along the whiskey bottle, a small icebox and a long-necked glass flask full of blood. She handed the drinks around. Blood and whiskey for the vampires; whiskey sours for herself and Xerxes. Xerxes accepted the drink gratefully and drank deeply. Across from him, Mina had already drank half of her glass.

There's definitely something in the air tonight, Xerxes thought coldly. *It isn't every night one hears that one's species is threatened with extinction. And from the most ironic source of all—from inside, not from the vampire hunters.*

Mina finished her drink. While Mildred fixed her another one, the vampires questioned Xerxes: "Are you certain of the time it'll take him to become contagious? We'll need to get him before then."

He nodded. He'd done some research on this and was certain of his facts: "Well, the old tomes say two weeks. But in the interests of safety and of unknown factors accelerating River's degeneration, assume just one week."

"One week," Mina growled. "And, with Max here, it couldn't have happened at a worse time."

"I'm sure the old guy'll understand once we explain the situation to him," Nick said.

The rest of the meeting was taken up with deciding the best way to apprehend River.

"It'll be safest to capture him during the day," Xerxes pointed out. "He'll be asleep then; or at least weak and tired."

"So will we," Mina countered. "We're all vampires."

Xerxes nodded. "Yes, yes, but your team can take a stimulant to keep them alert for a while."

Nick nodded too. "Yeah, from what you've told us, he won't expect us to be gunning for him. We walk in, slip him into a reinforced coffin and cart him away to a disposal site with an incinerator."

"Besides, I gave River some sleeping pills to handle the insomnia he complained of. He should be out cold when you arrive in his bedroom."

"At night, we could fly in," Mina still objected. Xerxes understood her aversion to doing anything in the daytime. When she spoke, her eyes reflected the bloodsucker's primal dread of going outside during the day. To a vampire, the sun was the true enemy, a force to be dreaded. It was feared more than River's impossible affliction, but for similar reason: the slightest caress of the sun's rays on a vampire's skin turned it to ash. Xerxes read Mina Cupples' thoughts in her eyes: *Two century's worth of unending pleasure and beauty burnt away in the twinkling of an eye. Nothing, not even the end of the world, was worth that.* He sympathized with her. For a woman, having one's looks instantly stripped away had to be the ultimate horror.

Nick Anderson sipped his whiskey-and-blood drink and set the glass down. If he was worried about a daytime operation; he concealed it very well. "There *is* one detail we need to handle tonight though," he said slowly.

"What's that?" Mina asked. She was on her fourth drink now.

"We need to get the capture team into the nightclub tonight."

Mina considered that for a moment, then said, "Yeah, you're right. Who do you have in mind for the job?"

"Annabelle and Marty—who both just started working there—Jack, and Pale Joe. And a backup crew of human associates. The

52

humans can arrive tomorrow morning to deliver something for Max. They'll have River's exit casket with them."

"You're doing this very quickly," Xerxes noted just to make conversation. Where strategy was concerned, there was little he could add. Beside him, Mildred noted the operatives' names down.

"The sooner the better," Mina agreed, waving her emptied glass at Mildred for a refill. "Personally, it's not something I want to keep having to think about." Then she frowned. "Nick, darling, I'm not sure Pale Joe's the right man to lead this operation."

Nick shrugged. "I don't see what can go wrong with it. In Joe's case, he's got additional motivation—he's coveted River's position for ages. Well, this provides him with a chance to prove he's worthy of it."

"Maybe you or I should do it instead."

"No, it might seem strange to River if one of us insisted on staying the night at the club; something we've never done before. But except for Jack, the others are there already for the party."

That seemed to settle it. Mildred poured fresh drinks for everyone and they tried to relax.

"So do you feel up to attending the party now?" Nick asked Mina a while later.

She shook her head. "It'll be impossible for me to act calm tonight. Let's just go home."

He nodded and got up. Xerxes shook his hand, and then he and Mildred escorted the vampire couple back upstairs to the roof, where after once again transforming into giant bats, they took to the air again and departed into the night like mobile shadows.

The doctor and his assistant watched them flap away.

"She's drunk too much again," Mildred noted of the smaller of the two vampire bats. "She's having trouble flying in a straight line. And she keeps bobbing up and down as if she'll drop out of the air at any moment."

Xerxes laughed. "Let's hope she doesn't. One should never drink and fly."

With Mildred too laughing at the joke, the pair of them returned downstairs to his office. In the elevator, Xerxes's mood was, if not reassured, then more settled than earlier. At least now something was being done about the impending crisis.

CHAPTER 11

Friday Night Fever

The party was a roaring success. Lots of fun and dancing. Lots of bloody alcohol to drink. Lots of food too: blood cake, blood pies and blood candy, though just like in humans, sugar tended to rot vampire teeth.

Music was provided by the vampire jazz quartet Heidi and the Bloodsuckers; who, since Max King was a huge fan (and onetime friend) of Old Blue Eyes, played mostly Frank Sinatra tunes. At one point, Heidi had the entire hall loudly singing "I drank her my way!"

In short, everyone had a ball and afterwards happily flew home to their beds or crypts. With no one the wiser to the plans the security agents had made for the next morning.

At about 4 a.m., when most of the guests had departed and Douglas River was having an intense drunken discussion with Max King, Pale Joe opened the rear door of the club to admit Jack Hill. Once Jack was inside the building, he and the other three members of the 'capture party' retired to Joe's suite on the second floor to conclude their preparations. Jack Hill handed around stimulant tablets designed to keep the vampires alert during their planned operation.

By the time they were through planning, it was daybreak. Satisfied that nothing could go wrong, the four retired to bed to get some sleep. All of them had set alarms to wake them at 9 a.m. Their attack was planned for 11 a.m. that Saturday morning, by which time Douglas River was certain to be fast asleep.

CHAPTER 12

River

Once again, River couldn't sleep. Though he now understood the cause of his insomnia, he still found it annoying, this unnatural disruption of a routine he'd kept for a century.

He lay in bed, fully clothed, more than a little drunk and with a hangover threatening to roar through his head at any moment.

All in all, he felt satisfied with himself. Everyone had enjoyed the party. Max King in particular, had been delighted.

River hadn't seen much of Alexia King; a group of her old friends had monopolized her all night. But that didn't matter, he'd liked what he had seen of her, and now that he seemed to be in her father's good books might be the right time to make a play for Alexia's morbid affections.

The only problem he'd had during the party was with drinking blood. Not with keeping the stuff down, but with maintaining an impassive expression when each drink he'd had had tasted increasingly awful.

But sleep . . . he turned to the nightstand, took a look at the sleeping pills Dr. Xerxes had given him. *Should I take them?* He decided not to. He felt there was something pathetic about a vampire requiring medication to get a good day's rest.

Instead, River got up, stripped off his clothes, and went to have a bath. *If I'm going to be human for a little while, I'd best start acting like one. I'm awake and I might as well show up at the office this morning.*

He was whistling as he brushed his teeth. After his bath, he got dressed. After noting that it was now 10:30 a.m., he exited the bedroom and headed for the second floor.

And that was why the four vampires missed River when they came to capture him.

CHAPTER 13

Capture Party

"Now, where the hell is he?" Pale Joe asked after the capture team stepped through River's bedroom door. The vampire was a tall and impressively muscular man with cropped black hair and corpse-white skin. "He should be asleep in here. That's what Mina said."

Annabelle Robinson walked over to River's left nightstand and picked up his bottle of sleeping pills. "Bottle's unopened," she pointed out. "He didn't take his medicine, meaning he's out and about somewhere, and wide-eyed awake. Which also means there's gonna be a fight."

"Shit!" Pale Joe said, slapping his palm with his 'wand'—a plastic rod which, once a stud on its side was depressed, projected a short bar of corrupted silver. The weapon worked like a stunner for vampires, the touch of the impure silver jolting them like an electric shock. All four members of the team were armed with the wands, which under ideal conditions should knock their target out easily.

Pale Joe grimaced. "Guys, this is supposed to be handled quietly, without any of the human staff knowing what's going on."

Jack Hill shrugged. "In that case, we shoulda taken him down last night, when they weren't around."

Joe shook his head. "That wouldn't have worked either. Mina and Nick wanna keep Max in the dark until this matter's been cleared up."

The fourth member of the capture team, Marty Collins, said nothing. He just stared around the room with something like jealousy in his cold eyes. Marty hadn't been a vampire for long and was impressed by the luxury River lived in.

Jack shook his head. "A quiet and unnoticed capture looks real unlikely now. Not with Max and his daughter right next door."

Annabelle gestured around the bedroom. "You gotta admit he's got great taste. Oh, what I wouldn't give for such luxury myself." While speaking, she gazed slyly at Pale Joe, knowing how much he envied River's position. But then, so did she.

Pale Joe gave no sign of noticing her insinuations. "Alright, we head downstairs," he said. "We'll check out his office first. If he ain't there, we'll all return here and wait for him to return."

CHAPTER 14

River

For a vampire some things were pleasant distractions. Like right now, when nightclub accountant Olivia Riley was bent over his desk, explaining to him why they'd overspent on wine purchases from Shields Demesne Winery during the previous month of September. Olivia was an attractive blonde, but her face and body weren't what River currently found so pleasing about her. No, Olivia was currently having her period. River could smell the blood flowing from her womb and staining her tampon. The reek of her made him both ecstatic and dizzy. She smelt so desirable, so delicious. It was all he could do not to bite her.

Not that he would anyway. He didn't mess with his employees. River sighed. Oh, but it would be so nice to sink his fangs into her.

". . . And so, sir," Olivia went on, "if we reduce the club purchases of Bloodroot and increase those of Roberts Run Red, we'll marginally increase profits, particularly as we approach the Christmas festivities, when everyone wants to have a good time."

"Yeah, but everyone prefers Bloodroot," River said. "That's the problem. "Listen, let's just leave things the way they are at the moment."

"Alright, sir. Now, the other thing we need to discuss is—"

A knock sounded on the office door,

River yawned, then called, "Come in."

It was the day manager Tony Petrelli. He looked rather hassled.

"What's up?" River asked Tony as the plump man sat on the couch by the glass wall. River's floor-to-ceiling office window was made of specially polarized glass, which only permitted the passage of light through it at night. Now, in daylight, the entire wall behaved like a mirror. River could see Tony and Olivia reflected in it; and also, very faintly, himself as well. His human companions, apparently, hadn't yet noticed that he was now visible.

"Ivy's car has been dumped," Tony said. "One of the ladies at last night's party helped drive it over to our disposal garage in Westover. I collected all of Ivy's personal effects from your bedroom and sent them off with her car, so that'll be the last of that."

"Good," Olivia said. "That car was an eyesore."

River said, "You look tired, Tony, what's with you?"

Tony forced a smile. "Nothing much, man. It's just the damn effort of single-handedly cleaning up all that spilled blood downstairs in the dancehall. You know I gave all our waitresses the morning off."

"Wasn't your new assistant—Annabelle—supposed to give you a hand with it?" Olivia asked.

"Yeah," River agreed. "I remember you telling me that she'd promised to stay awake and help you clean up."

Tony looked confused. "That's why I'm here now, man. I can't find Annabelle anywhere. I checked her bedroom—she's got this fairytale princess casket she sleeps in?—but she ain't inside it. Same thing for Marty the new guy too. I can't find either of them."

On hearing this, River felt a slight trickle of dread run down his spine. He didn't understand why he felt like this, but he sensed something was wrong. But then, the pleasant odor of the menstrual blood trickling into Olivia Riley's tampon dissolved his worries.

"Maybe Annabelle and Marty both forgot about you and flew off with the others," Olivia suggested. "Hey, listen, once I finish up here, I'll come give you a hand with cleanup."

Tony nodded. "Thanks, I'll appreciate that." He got up to leave and opened the office door. "Alright, you guys, I'm heading back to work. Lemme know if you see either Annabelle or Marty—"

"They're right here," a voice interrupted Tony. Then a brawny white hand shoved the fat man back into the room.

61

River sat up as Pale Joe strode into his office.

Pale Joe pushed Tony back down on the couch and said, "Sit there and mind your fucking business."

Behind Joe were the missing Annabelle Robinson and Marty, and another vampire whom after a few moments River recognized as Jack Hill. It was Hill's presence here that convinced River that he was in a shitload of trouble. Hill was vampire police; a ruthless fellow who took intense pride in tracking down vampire criminals and also in exterminating humans who'd become too much of a pest.

If he's here now . . . I'm in a shitload of trouble. And all four of them are holding wands. But what on earth have I done?

The answer to his question wasn't long in coming:

"Looks like it's the end of the fucking road for you, River," Pale Joe said.

"What's the charge?" River got to his feet, already alert to the wands each vampire bore with them. He glanced desperately around his office for something that might serve as a weapon.

Pale Joe beat his wand in his palm and shrugged. "I'm not exactly sure what you've done, but the order is to exterminate you before you can do any more of it." While he spoke Annabelle forced Olivia to sit on the couch beside Tony and hushed her with a finger across her lips.

River looked around at the other three vampires. All their faces were impassive, cold as ice. No sympathy. No mercy. Just their sense of him as a danger to be eradicated.

"Without a trial? Don't I get to state my case before the Vampire Council?"

"Sorry, boss, your sentence has already been passed. You're on a one-way trip from here to the nearest incinerator."

River could see that his assistant was doing his utmost best not to show how pleased he was at this abrupt reversal of their fortunes. River was clearly on his way down; Pale Joe on his way up.

"Alright, guys, take him," Pale Joe instructed. "Use the rods if he puts up a fight."

River quickly stepped behind his chair, lifted it up and flung it. He'd aimed the missile at Jack Hill, whom he considered the most dangerous of his opponents, but Hill quickly sidestepped and the airborne chair hit Marty the newbie flush in the face. Marty uttered a squawk and went down. He didn't get up again.

That was better, River thought. One down, three to go. He didn't consider himself much of a fighter, but when the alternative was being incinerated, his survival instinct automatically kicked into overdrive.

His attackers had to step around his desk to reach him and this gave him some space in which to maneuver. His office, however, had no other exit. The wall on his right was plasterboard, the one on his left glass with the sun outside, beside which Tony and Olivia sat with mixed expressions of fear and interest on their faces.

Pale Joe was the first vampire to reach River. He grabbed River's arm and jabbed the wand—with its silver prod extended—right into his neck. River howled from the pain of the contact, but then he realized he'd reacted more from fear than from the actual pain he'd experienced. In truth, the silver, which would have stunned a real vampire, hadn't hurt him that much. It had merely stung his neck.

Pale Joe didn't know this, however, and keeping the silver wand pressed against River's throat, he wrapped one of his massive arms around River's chest to keep him subdued. River played along while Jack Hill approached with his own wand extended, its protruded silver tip gleaming.

River waited until Jack Hill was right in front of him, then, still held in place by Pale Joe's steel grip, he leapt up and kicked Jack in the chest with both feet. Jack tumbled back over River's desk and vanished from sight.

Two down.

Pale Joe, however, now clubbed River over the head with his wand. The blow knocked River flat on the desk. He lay there stunned, gasping for air.

"Quick, Anna, the net!" Pale Joe called.

On hearing this call, River felt terrified. The net in question was built of woven steel and silver threads. No vampires could break out of its web and it reputedly felt like being burned in a fire.

River looked up, saw Annabelle about to cast the net at him, and rolled sideways to his right. The net landed where he'd been lying. River's roll had thrown him against Jack Hill, who'd just gotten up again and had been about to pin him to the desk. Before Jack could grab him, River picked up the net, and, spinning around, cast it over Jack's head. Jack howled in pain as he flung the net away from himself.

But River's little resistance was over. The next thing River knew, Jack Hill had recovered and was pressing the blade of a long serrated knife against his neck, digging it through his skin.

"One more move out of you, asshole," Jack said, baring his fangs, "and I'll behead you right here."

Pale Joe once more grabbed River from behind. "Alright, boss, time to go meet your maker. Anna, the net!"

River thought desperately. Once they got the net around him, he was finished. It was over. He'd be burnt up and forgotten before evening. He imagined that there was a human backup crew downstairs right now waiting to cart him away.

Then he realized he had an edge over the vampires and began laughing.

Annabelle had retrieved the net. "What are you laughing at?" she asked. "What can you possibly find funny about this?"

"You guys," River said. "You're all about to die."

"What?"

"Bye, guys," he said, "try not to get sunburnt."

Annabelle's eyes opened in shock. "What are you blabbing about?"

But River was already in motion, flinging himself at the reflective glass wall. As he saw his reflection nearing in it, he prayed it wasn't strong enough to resist his weight. Pale Joe was still holding onto him. Too bad for Pale Joe; good for himself as it increased the burden the glass had to withstand.

"NOOOO!" Pale Joe screamed when he realized what River intended to do. He tried to pull River back, but River was powered by a desperation to remain alive that Joe was powerless to resist. He held fast to Pale Joe when the frightened man let go of him, and dragged him to his fiery fate.

The two of them hit the glass wall. The glass shattered and both of them fell through it in a rain of shards.

River heard loud screams behind them as they fell, then he and Pale Joe hit the parking lot hard. Pale Joe landed on top of him. River felt a splitting pain in his left forearm as it took the brunt of their fall. But after a moment, he managed to roll Pale Joe off him and get to his feet and examine himself.

I gambled and it paid off, he thought with satisfaction.

His skin felt hot, as hot as if he was on fire, but his body wasn't smoking. But he'd suffered a broken arm—part of one of his left forearm bones had torn through his skin.

Still, standing there in the bright morning sunlight—daylight he'd not seen for a century—he had the feeling that he'd be alright.

He couldn't say the same for Pale Joe though. The two-floor fall hadn't hurt the vampire, but the sun had. Joe was on fire, burning from his hair to his shoes; his clothes an eruption of flames, his skin boiling and flaking off as River watched. Howling with horror and pain, Pale Joe got to his feet, and tried to stumble towards the club's side entrance. But then one of his knees seemed to explode, and he crashed down on the concrete again. And then his head exploded too, his brains spilling across the parking lot in shriveling hot lumps. His remains withered away, crumpling to ash.

River glanced up at his shattered office window. The smoke spilling from it meant that at least one more of his vampire attackers had suffered the same fate as Pale Joe. Maybe Marty, who'd been knocked out by the chair he'd thrown.

Then, realizing that even if the sun wouldn't kill him, the human backup crew might still capture him, which would amount to the same thing, River turned away from the Haven club and hurried off through the nearby woods.

He realized he needed to find another safe haven and fast.

CHAPTER 15

Crystal . . . That Afternoon

"So, who the hell is Max King?" Crystal asked her housemate while they crossed the parking lot to the Haven club to start their afternoon shift.

"Your guess is as good as mine. Probably some long-tooth big shot."

Josie had sent an email query to this effect to the VEINS server but hadn't yet gotten a reply. Nor, harking back on personal experience, did the girls expect to receive one anytime soon. The people who ran the VEINS organization certainly had to pay their bills too, and Josie's email would most likely be number 200th in line to need attending to when whoever checked the organization's messages got around to doing so.

"At the moment you and I are completely on our own," Crystal pointed out. "And that's not our fault, but the system's."

She wasn't placing the blame, just stating the facts. The vampire society was rich and powerful, and also well-organized up through the various levels of American society. In its unseen intrusive way, it even managed to influence government policy. To combat this menace, the creators of VEINS (which had both fewer people and fewer resources) had gone the opposite route in setting up their vampire-strike organization. In sharp contrast to the vampires' well-organized setup, VEINS was anything but. VEINS was completely decentralized. It was nebulous and as such untraceable. VEINS had web servers through which its members could communicate, but all such communications

67

were anonymous. Most VEINS members were unaware of each other's involvement in the worldwide vampire eradication project.

Crystal considered their own situation a case in point. The VEINS cells worked in partnership pairs. She and Josie were a pair. Each pair was aware of only one other pair with whom they shared a higher-up contact. That higher-up individual was the pair's only connection to the central organization. She and Josie's contact had been Donny Smith.

"The system's all well and good until your contact dies and you're cut adrift," Josie said.

"Yeah," Crystal agreed. "Now, Donny's dead, killed in last night's attack, and we've something really big going on here and no one to report it to."

"It might be even bigger than that," Josie said, pointing towards the front of the Haven building, where a black and white squad car was just pulling out of the parking lot onto Easton Mill Road. "The cops were just here. I wonder why."

The pair clocked in, were told by manager Tony Petrelli (who looked both extremely nervous and overworked) that the club would be closed that evening and night, and were then assigned by him to clean up the mess in River's office.

***

Crystal and Josie quickly found out from one of the other waitresses why the police had visited. Apparently, a concerned passerby had reported seeing a man burning in the club's parking lot. The passerby had also reported seeing a second man running off into the nearby woods and had noticed too that one of the building's second floor windows had been shattered.

In River's office itself, there were two piles of ash on the floor and objects scattered everywhere as there had been a fight. The window as a jagged mess, with long suspended shards projecting into the middle space like translucent glass teeth. Almost all the broken glass had fallen outside into the parking lot.

"I really wonder what Tony told the cops when they saw this," Josie said as she swept up the vampire ash into a dustpan.

"An attempted robbery, no doubt. Definitely not the truth." She scrubbed at a greasy spot with a brush.

"I wonder who got fried outside," Crystal said, peering down through the shattered window at the black smear down on the concrete.

Josie looked around to make sure no one was in earshot, before replying. "I dunno, but the one who ran off sounds like River."

"So he got away then."

The last of the vampire ash swept up, the two young woman got to work retrieving the scattered stationary and rearranging it on the desk.

"Three dead vamps," Crystal said. "There's certainly gonna be a vampire conference about this."

Josie nodded. "And if it takes place in Xerxes's office, we're gonna be listening in."

Crystal surveyed River's office. It looked alright, except of course for the shattered glass wall and the pair of damp patches on the floor.

"I think it's fine," Josie said. "Look, Crys, let's see if they need us for anything else or if we can go home. I think it's time we had our own conference."

Crystal nodded. Together they pushed the cleanup cart towards the elevator.

The manager didn't need them for anything else. Mr. Petrelli and the accountant Ms. Riley were both deep in conference and didn't appear to have time for anyone.

"OK, you're done with it? Yes, goodbye then. See you both Monday morning," was the manager's curt reply to their inquiry.

"This gets stranger and stranger," Crystal told Josie as they exited into the cool autumn afternoon. "Tony and Olivia look like they both saw the same ghost."

"Or like they both saw the same ghost catch fire," Josie agreed.

At home a short while later, and with coffees in hand to burn away the chill of the day, Crystal and Josie listened again to the third recording they'd gotten from Dr. Xerxes's office the previous night.

"So what're we gonna do now?" Josie asked afterwards. "From what we've just listened to and what we saw at work, it's clear that the vamps went after River, but something went wrong and he got away. But we gotta do something."

"I need to think," Crystal said. Josie was the more effervescent member of their pairing; the more action-oriented one. She, on the other hand, did all their planning. Josie was an in-the-moment person; she just didn't have the patience for reasoning stuff out.

Crystal let her mind rove over their options.

"We should ask Jerry and Sheila over for a group conference," Josie suggested a minute later.

"No need, and besides it's too dangerous. Someone from work might recognize Jerry and get suspicious." Jerry Foley (who, along with his wife Sheila comprised the only other VEINS pair that the girls knew) worked at the BSS clinic as their communications technician. He'd installed the bug in the doctor's intercom.

"Or, maybe we can do a webcam chat," Josie suggested.

"Drink your damn coffee and let me think!" Crystal growled at her. "Or play a game on your cellphone."

She was relieved that Josie seemed to take her advice. She pulled out her Samsung Galaxy and began fiddling with it.

Crystal now tried to give her full attention to the problem facing them. What should they do now? But instead of coming up with an answer, she found that her mind kept pulling her back in time to the insane night that she'd gotten involved with VEINS.

***

That Saturday night three years ago, Crystal Barkley was out clubbing at Float with her boyfriend Todd. They'd been dancing and having a great time. But then, at around midnight, Todd had said he needed to go pee and that he'd be right back. He'd left Crystal at their table, sipping water and nodding her head to the music.

Problem was, thirty minutes later, Todd still wasn't yet back from the toilets. Crystal assumed he'd met some old friends and was having a laugh with them. But when Todd still hadn't returned an hour after he'd left her, Crystal had grown very worried.

She'd gotten up and pushed her way through the dancers and walked towards the men's room. There was a long line of young men waiting to use the place, several of whom she knew. She'd asked them if they'd seen her boyfriend. Someone replied that, yes, he'd seen Todd leaving the club with another young man. He'd assumed Todd wanted to cop some drugs from the guy and thought nothing more of it. The other guy had looked like a junkie—pale skin, spaced-out eyes, and was really thin like he'd not eaten a good meal in weeks.

Perplexed, Crystal had thanked them, left the nightclub and gone to look for Todd outside.

She found Todd's motorbike still in the parking lot, meaning he'd not left the place; so he had to be around somewhere.

She'd walked around the Float club's building. The rear of the building was shaded in darkness, the security light on that side busted. It was here she'd found Todd. He was standing against the rear club wall. The other young man had his mouth clamped tightly to Todd's neck.

Crystal's first angry thoughts that the pair had come outside to have sex were quickly quashed when the other boy, on hearing her approach, lifted his lips from Todd's throat and glared at her. In the moonlight, she saw that his lips were red, dripping with blood, and that his canine teeth were extremely long. The rest of his face was strange too, his eyes terrifyingly bloodshot and his forehead thick and prominent with warped ridges of bone, his nose shrunken till it was almost nonexistent. His hair was black and long.

The young man scowled at her, blood dripping down his chin and onto his black jacket, and let go of Todd. Todd, who'd been motionless since Crystal's arrival on the scene, now slid slowly down the wall, his eyes wide and staring at nothing, two bright red lines trickling down his neck and collecting along the neckline of his white t-shirt. Crystal was certain that Todd was dead.

The horrible young man smiled. "See what a pretty little gift the night has brought me," he said and moved towards her. "Well, honey, let's have some of your blood too." His voice was unnaturally echoic, as if it had been fed through a sound-processing unit. He stretched a hand towards her and she saw that it was warped and hairy and had long black fingernails.

"No, no!" Crystal had gasped, finding herself both unable to scream and unable to run. She hadn't even known that she was pissing herself, her bladder letting go of all the night's drinks. The warm urine flooded out of her crotch and wet the insides of her leather pants, while she retreated in slow motion, with the monstrous creature who'd just murdered her boyfriend moving quickly towards her.

And then he'd grabbed her and grinned at her, his bloodshot eyes staring into hers and increasing her already intense terror.

"Please, don't kill me!" she'd pleaded, still unable to accept that this thing—this had to be a vampire, right?—was actually real.

The vampire hadn't answered. Instead, he'd forced her against the wall and bent his head towards her gulping throat.

Crystal tensed, expecting to feel the horrible fangs puncturing her flesh the next moment.

But right before that seemingly inescapable violation happened, she'd been rescued. Someone had pulled the vampire off of her.

Enraged, the young man had spun around to face those who'd interrupted his meal of blood.

Two young men and a young woman had now arrived on the scene. All were about Crystal's age, and though she didn't know any of them personally, she remembered seeing them inside the nightclub earlier. She thought one of the boys might have been in the line to use the men's toilets when she'd been asking after Todd's whereabouts. The girl—two or three inches taller than herself, brunette, and with a boyish haircut—was carrying a long brown leather case.

She was very grateful to be rescued. Even now, seeing the vampire's teeth snapping as he tried to bite the two young men who now had his arms pinned behind his back, she felt like screaming in terror.

"Who are you guys?" she asked.

The trio didn't reply to her, their attentions totally focused on their captive. The boys muscled him backward until his back was flat against the club wall. The girl meanwhile, had gotten out from her leather case a thin foot-long length of wood with one end sharpened to a point. She held this in one hand and picked up a wooden mallet with the other.

"Hey, Jake, how'd you like some stake for breakfast?" she'd next asked the vampire.

The vampire's eyes now showed signs of fear. "No, please!"

He'd made a violent move to throw off the young men holding his arms, and might have succeeded, but the girl quickly placed the sharp point of the wooden rod against his chest and smashed her mallet against its other end. As if sucked inside by a vacuum, the stake slid smoothly into the vampire's chest. The young man screamed at the agonizing penetration, then went limp, just as Todd had done.

"Let him go, you guys, he's finished."

Her companions dropped the vampire, who, even before he'd hit the floor, had begun smoking and crumpling to ash.

"You didn't get bit, did you?" one of the young men had asked Crystal.

Unable yet to trust herself to speak, she'd shaken her head back at him. She'd pressed herself close to the wall and watched her assailant disintegrate. By now she was too perplexed to be frightened. Something had quickly struck her as obvious though: the calm, self-assured way in which her rescuers had seemingly forgotten about the staked vampire—they hardly looked at it as it crumbled to nothingness—assured Crystal that they'd done this before, maybe more than once even.

And her trio of rescuers weren't done yet. Once satisfied that Crystal was unharmed, they'd turned their full attention to Todd, who was half-lying, half-sitting by the wall.

"Check him out, man," the taller of the two boys told the other. "See if he's still alive."

The other young man knelt by Todd and took his pulse. He did this twice, then spread Todd's eyelids and shone a flashlight into his pupils.

"Nah," he told the others. "He's a turner, for sure."

The girl had instantly gotten out a second stake from her leather case.

"Hey wait!" Crystal had protested as the girl advanced on Todd with grim intent in her eyes. "You can't do that to him!"

The girl didn't even look at her. "Yes I can and I'm going to."

Crystal tried to stop her, but one of the young men held her back. Sensing she was about to scream for help—she was—he clamped a meaty hand over her mouth. Crystal was forced to watch helplessly while the girl gave Todd the same treatment she'd given the vampire, which was now a white pile of ash on the concrete floor. Once more her mallet rose and descended and her wooden spike entered into flesh.

When she staked Todd, he let out a sharp yelp of agony and then instantly began disintegrating too, turning to ash.

"Let her go," the girl told the boy who was restraining Crystal. "I'm sure she'll believe her own eyes."

Crystal was released and ran to Todd's side. His skin and clothes were already flaking to the ground, his face collapsed in on itself to reveal a skull that fell apart as she watched. The ash fluttered away on the night breeze that had just whipped up. Pieces of Todd blew into her face, making her cough.

She couldn't even cry. She'd gotten up and turned to face the trio.

The girl extended her hand to Crystal. "Hi, I'm Josie and"—with a broad gesture she indicated her male companions—"these guys are Jerry and Donny."

Crystal nervously shook her hand. "Who are you guys?" She wasn't really looking at the other girl; her attention was riveted to the absurd and impossible spectacle before her: watching her boyfriend of barely an hour ago withering away into a pile of ash like he was a piece of burning cardboard.

"We're members of VEINS," Jerry replied.

"VEINS?" Crystal asked distractedly. "What the hell's that?"

Donny explained: "VEINS stands for Vampire Engagement, Investigation and Neutralization Syndicate."

"Oh, I see," Crystal replied. But all she could really see was that by now, both Todd and the vampire were completely gone; just ash trails remaining as proof that they'd ever existed. Whatever was she going to tell Todd's parents?

Then she realized that Josie was smiling brightly at her.

"What?" she asked, confused by the girl's abrupt attitude shift from dead serious to very friendly.

And then Josie had surprised her with a question: "Hey, so do you wanna join VEINS too?"

"What?"

"Well, after what you've just seen, you wanna join us and kick vampy butt too, don't'cha?"

"I-I-I dunno," Crystal replied as Josie linked her fingers with hers and led her back around to the front of the club building, the guys following behind them. "I just feel so confused right now."

"That's what everyone says at first," Josie replied with an amused smile on her face, "but they all get over it. Trust me on this—there's no rush like hunting down the undead."

***

No damn rush like hunting down the undead, Crystal thought, slowly resurfacing from her reverie. *Well, Josie certainly didn't lie about that. She and I have been kicking undead ass together for three years now and we make a great team. But the more vampires we kill, the more of them there seem to be. What we need is a comprehensive assault approach, something to take out all the vampires*

75

at one go, or at least so many of them that the rest will go into hiding, like in the good old days.

"You come up with anything yet?" Josie asked. "This damn game ain't letting me win today."

Crystal surfaced from her reverie to find Josie peering impatiently at her. For a moment she had no idea what to tell her friend, but then she was hit by burst of inspiration. An earth-shattering idea took up residence in her mind and refused to depart.

She sipped her coffee, trying to calm down and organize her thoughts. The drink had cooled during her reminiscence, which meant she'd been locked into her memories (with Josie just as locked into her phone game) for quite a while.

"Listen, Josie," she said finally, "I'm thinking here that to make a real difference in this human–vamp war we need to do something massive to break the deadlock."

"How do you mean, massive?"

"Well, killing the vampires one at a time like we keep doing is really just a waste of time. How many of them have you and I personally staked in the past three years? Fifteen?"

"More like twenty?"

"That many? And yet there's never a shortage of 'em. See what I mean? It's like culling deer during hunting season; next hunting season there's just as many deer as last year. Sure, VEINS keeps the vamps' numbers down, but they just need to bite more folks to death and then there's automatically more of 'em, see?"

Josie put her phone down and frowned. "No, I don't see. What are you suggesting we do instead?"

Crystal smiled. "River's the key. The vampires are clearly terrified of what he's got, right? So I propose that we help make their worst nightmares come true."

Josie frowned some more, but then she got it, her eyes brightening suddenly. "You're proposing that we find River before the vamps do and help him infect the other vampires with the humanitis disease?"

Crystal nodded. "Yeah, exactly that. You heard too what Xerxes and the woman said in the recording. Two weeks and River will be a time bomb to the vamps. It can't fail."

"So we find him and take him captive." But then her expression fell. "Shit, Crys, we don't have the tools to keep a vampire in quarantine. Neither we nor the Foleys even have a basement in our homes; so where are we supposed to keep River? No, this is too big for us to deal with. We need the organization to handle this."

Crystal shook her head. "We need to face the facts, girl. At the moment, until we either hear back from the VEINS server or they repair our downlink from the chain of command, *we are* the entire VEINS organization."

Josie shook her head too. "We can't capture River, Crys. If you were suggesting we find him and stake him, I'd agree with you, but . . ."

"But we *can't* stake him, that's the problem. What's he's infected with is too valuable to us. We need the sonofabitch alive and well."

"Easy to say, but we don't even know where he is."

"Neither do the vampires," Crystal quickly pointed out. "But they'll be desperately searching for him; we can both rest assured of that. We just need to keep listening in on their conversations." Then she grinned at Josie. "And you, girl, you need to keep sucking Pete the Security Guy's dick . . . or whatever you were doing so efficiently two days ago that seems to have made him fall in love with you."

"Hell no," Josie said, shaking her palms at Crystal. "Not that slob. You do it."

Crystal rolled her eyes. "I would, but you lost our coin toss that day. And besides, he prefers brunettes anyway. Girl, I'm not asking you to fall in love with him. Just fuck him for info. Just till they catch River; then you can break up with him. Both Pete and that other security guy Claudio are vampire collaborators, they're certain to know all the latest news about the chase."

"I'll do it if you're screwing Claudio at the same time," Josie said.

"We can't double-date them, or rather double-fuck them," Crystal patiently pointed out. "It'll look suspicious. If we're both asking them the same questions, they'll quickly figure out that we're using them."

"Oh alright," Josie agreed. "And you? While I'm sacrificing my pussy to help us win the human–vamp war, what'll you be doing?"

"I'll ensure you have enough condoms," Crystal said sweetly. "We don't want you getting pregnant with Pete's baby now, do we?"

Josie gave her the finger. Crystal smirked back at her, relieved that the matter had been settled. Josie left the living room. Crystal stretched out on the couch and tried to figure out a way to trap and hide River until he became infectious.

If we can find him before the vamps do, that is. She frowned. *I wonder where the hell he is now anyway?*

CHAPTER 16

River

River was very angry.

Once out of sight of the Haven club, River had crossed the road and then kept under the trees. He'd quickly discovered that his immunity to sunlight was only partial. He didn't think it could melt or explode him, but just a few minutes exposure seemed to give him sunburn, turning his skin lobster-orange and making it peel and flake off like old lizard skin. Under the trees the damage reversed.

River felt intense rage. He couldn't believe the Vampire Society could betray him like this.

That bastard Xerxes lied to me! But why?

This was a puzzle that he understood he had no time to ponder. He was very conscious of pursuit, very conscious of the need to conceal himself now, not just from the Vampire Society, but also from humans who might think him suspicious and call the police to investigate.

The main problem with that was that the police department was full of vampire associates. One phone call from some scared woman who'd noticed him walking through her yard was all it would take for River to be arrested. And then he'd not be thrown into a police cell. No, seeing as he'd committed no actual crime, the cops would nicely insist on returning him to the nightclub, which was as good as a death sentence.

So now I'm a damned fugitive!

Keeping beside Cheat Road so he didn't get lost, River paused under a large oak tree to attend to his left arm. The pain from the fracture was keeping him from focusing. A quick examination of the wound revealed that while he might be turning human, he still had a lot of vampire in him. The torn flesh had already ceased bleeding and was trying to seal itself up, the one obstruction to this being the broken bone projecting through the skin.

River pushed the projecting shaft of bone back through the hole it had torn in his flesh. While doing so, he made an effort not to yell with pain. But still, once he'd concluded the action, he needed a few seconds to recover himself. After this short pause he did his best to realign the bone correctly with its other half.

Pain. Shit. That's a major downside to turning human.

He remained sitting on the grass for a while, letting the bone heal itself. The torn forearm skin was already repaired, and he could feel the ends of bone knit together too. He wondered how long this healing ability would last though.

I need to be really careful from now on. No more crazy stunts.

He looked around, trying to decide which way to go. The oak beneath which he'd taken refuge was quite wide and totally hid him from the sight of any motorists coming along Cheat Road. The immense tree had already lost a good number of leaves to the fall season and lost a few more as he sat beneath it. So far so good. About fifty yards down the road was the last house he'd passed, and peeking through the woods ahead, he thought he could make out a few more buildings. He wasn't used to this area in the daytime–that was the thing.

Behind him were the thick woods that lead back to the nightclub.

He was staring out at the road, wondering which way to go and trying to keep his anger at his betrayal in check, when he spotted the police cruisers. Two vehicles emerging from the Army Band Way junction, which most likely meant that they were coming from the Haven club. River ducked back into cover. He felt very alarmed. So, the search was already on for him then.

What are the society gonna tell the cops? Yeah, I know they'll tell them I went berserk and attacked Pale Joe and the others and then ran off. Shit!

Back in concealment, River could no longer see the road, but he suddenly became aware of footsteps heading his way. And loud male voices.

"Hey, Mike, are you absolutely certain you saw someone in here amongst these damn trees?"

"Yeah, I'm sure, man. Might be the club robber. Our caller said he saw the guy heading into the forest in this direction."

"Alright, but keep your eyes peeled for copperheads."

An intense surge of vampire anger, anger at being hunted down like an animal filled River. For a moment he was tempted to come out of cover, to reveal himself to the two policemen, to attack them, to rend their human flesh to shreds and drink their sweet blood wine.

But he controlled himself. Even though his arm had just successfully healed itself he didn't wish to discover if his body could repair bullet wounds too. And also, he realized that acting irrationally now—giving in to his anger—wouldn't help him in the least. At the moment, his only real enemies were his own people. The Vampire Society were the only ones after him. The WV police had no reason to hunt him down. But that would surely change in an instant if he foolishly killed these two approaching police officers.

So instead, River sneaked away into the trees ahead. It helped that the two cops had lost their bearing amongst the trees and were headed away to his left.

"Hey, I can see movement through the trees over there. That's him over there! Hey, you, wait!"

"Shit, Mike, you need to get your eyes tested! That's a damn animal. A fox or a bear."

River didn't even realize that they were referring to him. He had no idea that in his flight, he'd instinctively transformed into wolf shape. He only realized this when he was a hundred yards away from the police officers and trotting even deeper into the woods.

When he did realize what he'd done, he was relieved that at least he still had this vampire ability. It should prove useful in the dangerous days ahead.

But then the wolf instinct took over and all he knew was running. Racing between trees, dashing across roads, and running at breakneck speed over a wide body of water, moving so fast that the gray wolf was almost invisible to the five or six vehicles on the bridge during its transit . . .

CHAPTER 17

Dr. Xerxes & the Vampire Society

That Saturday night another meeting was held in Arnold Xerxes's office. Mina Cupples and Nick Anderson were in attendance, and also Max and Alexia King. Once again, Mildred sat in as recorder.

"You could just have called, sir, and we'd have come over to the Haven club," Xerxes had protested to Max King after the vampires had alighted on the BSS Clinic's rooftop and transformed back to human form. "No need to trouble yourself with coming over."

The vampire leader had laughed, revealing ancient fangs the color of old ivory. "No trouble at all. I like to get out every now and again." Though he mostly spoke very proper English, he had something of a southern accent. 'And besides, I've heard a great deal of good things about your establishment here, doctor. I'd already planned to visit you before I left town. It's a great honor to finally meet one of our greatest associates and helpers."

Xerxes bowed humbly. "Believe me, sir, the honor is all mine."

Xerxes led the vampires to his elevator. "And thanks for the virgins' blood," Alexia remarked as they rode the cage down to the 2nd floor. "Dad can't get enough of it. I think the real reason he insisted on coming over was so he could talk some more of it out of you."

Max King was tall and cadaverous, looking every minute of his thousand-plus years. There was nothing attractive about him. His gaze reflected an evil lust, his posture and attitude was proud and superior. Max King's black suit looked almost as old as he did. Xerxes couldn't tell if the ancient vampire's faint reek of decay was because his clothes were moldy or if that was his natural odor.

King's daughter Alexia though, was a different kettle of fish altogether.

Alexia King looked about thirty-five years old. She had blonde hair and green eyes and was very thin, almost like a catwalk manikin, with her blue jeans and brown blouse dangling loosely off her body. Sexy in a trashy kind of way. The 'young' woman shared her father's jaded look, however.

He seated the vampires in his office. Mildred had already mixed blood cocktails for everyone.

"This whole River business is a very nasty one," King said after a sip of his drink. "Personally, I like the kid—he's done really good keeping this state running smoothly, but . . ." He spoke with an assured attitude, but Xerxes sensed an undercurrent of fear underlying the vampire patriarch words.

"It's a real mess," Alexia said. "So now we've gotta kill River before he kills all of us?" Her attitude and behavior were completely modern; she could be a rich human socialite or some billionaire's spoilt and wasted daughter—which, truth be told, wasn't very far from the truth.

"More or less," Mina Cupples agreed. Tonight, she'd barely touched her drink. Xerxes realized that Mina was aware that the vampire's doomsday clock was ticking, the countdown timer running fast down to zero. This wasn't any time for alcoholic indulgence. "This morning's operation should have taken care of everything. But we never considered that his sleep patterns had already become completely human." She sounded worried too, aware that the blame for letting the fugitive get away could easily be put on herself and Nick. Nick, so far wasn't saying anything, was just looking moody.

Max King waved Mina's worries away. "Not everything can be planned for," he said. "And we're not here to apportion blame. What is important now, is that we find River . . . and fast at that." The old vampire peered closely at Xerxes. "How long do you say we have before he turns toxic to us?"

"A week. Two at most," Xerxes promptly replied. "There is one old fable that gives a window of two months, but I wouldn't dare place any bets on its reliability. Everything else I've been able to dig up pegs the contagion offset for humanitis to a fortnight at best."

Max King nodded slowly. "Two weeks, or the house of cards comes crumbling down."

Alexia King was seated right beside Xerxes. "Have you had any luck with finding a potential cure?" she asked him. She smelt nice too, of lemon and roses mingled with just the faintest hint of decay. A scent of beauty and danger.

"I'm working on it," he replied to her.

"Any progress so far?" she insisted.

"Well, I don't wish to raise any false hopes, so I'd best say no to that. But please rest assured that I and my assistants are doing our utmost to find a cure. We're working with the sample of blood I took from River. It's slow work—first we need to isolate the specific agent responsible for his reversal—but I'm confident that with a little luck, we'll be able to crack it."

Max King nodded approvingly at Xerxes. "You keep doing that, son, and we'll keep looking for River."

Xerxes thought he now understood how Max King had remained vampire leader for so long: the old man's calm was unparalleled. Maybe it was because King was supposedly over a millennium old. Some claimed that his age was closer to two millennia, that 'Max' actually stood for 'Maximus,' that he'd been a Roman general at the time Christ was crucified. It was known for certain that he was the oldest vampire in the USA. He'd been staked more than once but had had had the good fortune to be resurrected by magical ritual over and over again.

Xerxes absentmindedly wondered how old Alexia King was: Five hundred years? Seven hundred? She was watching him intently now, with a familiar twinkle in her green eyes.

Aw, come on. She's not interested in me, is she?

He smiled politely back at her. He found her wasted rock groupie charm attractive. He was single; had never married. Knowing his future, Xerxes hadn't wanted the burden of a family. Most women he'd dated would have loved his wedding ring on their finger, and he'd definitely been tempted to tie the knot more than once, but he could never escape the knowledge that someday he'd need to leave the woman and his children behind to enter the dark undead realm for good. And even while married there would be nothing except secrets between them. Layers and layers of secrets, which sooner or later would drive the wedge of divorce between them.

A weak excuse. You enjoy being single. If not, you could easily marry one of the female vampire associates. Like Mildred, for instance.

Mildred Wilson was divorced; her two children living with her ex. Though Mildred claimed otherwise, Xerxes suspected that his secretary's marriage had broken up for the very reason that he was wary of tying the knot: that burgeoning web of untruths which must surely unravel one day, if for no other reason than the fact that sooner or later one's spouse would feel compelled to investigate one's strange associates and the stranger still hours one kept, even without the suspicion that a romantic affair was being conducted behind their backs.

He stole a gaze at Mildred, wondering how she was coping with being single again. She'd recently begun dating someone over at the Haven club. She noticed him watching her and smiled back.

Closer to home, Xerxes realized that Alexia King was still watching him with interest. So that confirmed it: she *was* interested in him. A beautiful complication, but one for later.

He looked away from her, concentrated on what Nick Anderson was saying.

Despite the grim severity of the issue at hand, Xerxes found it difficult to stop his thoughts drifting. He understood that this meeting was being held in his office because of the need for secrecy. Seeing someone going to the doctor instantly created the mental impression that the person was ill, not that they were conducting a police investigation. So yes, his office *was* the ideal place to meet. But other than the odd medical detail, Xerxes had nothing to contribute here.

". . . This means that River must still be within the neighborhood," Nick said.

Mina nodded her agreement. "The main thing we've got in our favor is that River still has no real idea of exactly *why* we're after him. We don't expect him to keep running though. We can be certain he'll want to find out why we're trying to kill him before leaving town. That and the fact that all his personal items—cellphone, credit cards etc.—are still in the nightclub, and he'll need them to go anywhere. The direction in which he headed on leaving the club would place him near I-68, which, if he hitched a ride or stole a car, would take him east into Maryland, or even up into Pennsylvania if he switched to Route 43 in Cheat Lake . . . but he's more likely to just hole up somewhere nearby. Maybe even hide out in the woods."

Xerxes was impressed by Mina's professionalism tonight. She was still only halfway through her first whiskey and blood, and completely unrecognizable as the party animal of the previous night.

Max King stroked his craggy jaw. "So what do the two of you propose doing?" he asked.

"We wait," Nick said. "Wait for him to screw up and reveal where he's hiding."

"Wait?" Alexia asked. "Isn't that a little irresponsible with time running out so fast?"

Mina stared at Alexia with some dislike. "No, it isn't irresponsible. We'll keep our eyes and ears open, of course, and our police associates will too." Then she either relented in her anger over Alexia's suggestion of her incompetence, or merely decided that with the woman's exalted father present, a continued demonstration of that anger would prove counterproductive to her career interests, because she visibly simmered down and explained sweetly: "View it this way, Alexia: River is bound to do something very silly very soon. Yes, he's smart, but he's also very impulsive and quite easily moved to anger."

"He'll also be very scared now, and unsure who he can trust," Nick added. "He knows we're looking for him and that we're gonna kill him when we do catch him."

"He's like a wounded lion; strong but helpless," Mina finished. "You can be certain that very soon he'll be on the news for something stupid he's done. But meanwhile, we'll keep our eyes and ears open too."

Xerxes felt he should say something too, and so added: "I agree with Mina and Nick. A waiting game is our best bet. For all we know, River may even be so dumb as to come here to settle the score with me for deceiving him."

"Sounds reasonable enough to me," Max King said. He looked pointedly at his daughter. "We'll stay off their backs and let them do their jobs." He turned his sepulchral smile on Xerxes. "And now, doctor, I'd like a tour through your establishment. And more virgin's blood, of course," he added with a laugh.

That essentially ended the meeting. After a final round of drinks for everyone, Mildred cleared the glasses and bottles away, while Xerxes led the vampires out for a tour of the clinic complex.

"I must admit I'm very impressed," the vampire leader said an hour later, as the elevator cage bore the five of them up to the rooftop. He patted Xerxes fondly on the back. "You've a wonderful setup here, son, keep up the good work."

"We try our best," Xerxes humbly replied. In the cramped metal cage, the old vampire's moldy smell was stifling him, like he was suffocating on fumes of raw age, heady but sickening. And on Xerxes's other side, Alexia King was showing her own fondness for him, covertly rubbing her breasts and crotch against him while leaning on his shoulder.

"Yeah, it's a really great setup you've got going here, doc," Alexia said. "Seeing all that refrigerated blood almost had me dizzy with delight."

"I'll have some more of it sent over for you tomorrow," Xerxes told father and daughter as the cage ground to a halt on the roof. He stepped out of it with relief, with Alexia now seemingly glued to his side. Max King walked off ahead of them all to stare over the rooftop at the city lights. Mina and Nick walked behind Xerxes and Alexia, discussing something in low voices.

"Hey, man, be here tomorrow night at this same time," Alexia whispered into Xerxes's ear after licking and nipping it gently with her fangs. "There's a few things I wanna discuss with you."

"Yes, sure," Xerxes whispered back, but she didn't see or hear his response. She was already walking off to join her father at the edge of the roof, her skinny form swaying like the slight wind would blow it over.

"She likes you a lot," Mina said, stepping up next to Xerxes. "Better watch out that she doesn't wear your dick down to the nub. I don't think the old girl's been laid in twenty years."

Xerxes tried not to blush. He walked with Mina and Nick to join Max and Alexia King. He and Max shook hands, and then he stepped back, while the vampires transformed and took to the sky.

Oh, how wonderful and glorious, Xerxes thought as the four giant bat-creatures rose up into the night, their immense black wings blocking the stars from view. He watched the evil creatures fly off for a while, imagining the day when he'd do likewise, then turned and reentered the elevator to go continue his work on analyzing River's blood to separate the humanizing element it contained.

CHAPTER 18

River

River woke up. It was night.

River had no idea of when he'd fallen asleep. In wolf form, he'd travelled any number of miles, before, feeling exhausted, he given himself up to slumber. He remembered being near a town; but in animal form, with the intellect subdued and the animal mind in ascendency, he'd been unable to determine which of Morgantown's neighboring communities it was. The sun had been high at the time, its hot rays seeming to penetrate deep through the leafy cover. The wolf had crawled under a heavy pile of brush and autumn leaves and had passed out.

Sometime during its slumber, the wolf had become a man again.

And now it was nighttime. And he was awake and due to the exertions of his flight, he was very hungry. The hunger burnt in him like fire.

He needed blood, plenty of it.

River pulled himself out from under the brush pile and dusted himself off. He had twigs and leaves in his hair and even in his pockets.

Once he'd cleaned himself off enough, he tried to figure out where he was. *Yeah, I saw a town nearby, but in what direction?*

He had no idea. The moon was out now, large and brilliant in the sky and he could see around him for a distance, but all he saw were trees in various stages of losing their leaves. He caught flashes of movement amidst the trees; wood creatures who'd either come to investigate his presence or whom his presence had scared off.

But the hunger! His need for food clawed at his guts like an animal eating them. A red haze filled his mind. *Blood! I need blood!* The need to feed seemed to take over his intelligence.

He was scarcely aware of when he transformed into a bat and leapt up into the night, his massive wings shattering the branches of several trees as he passed them.

And then he was free, high above the forest, a starving monster seeking human prey.

CHAPTER 19

Tammy

"Open the door, Tammy. It's daddy!"

14-year-old Tammy Young cringed at the drunken request, one that she'd come to dread. She lay in bed in her upstairs room with the covers drawn up to her neck, staring at her locked bedroom door like it was a monster that wanted to eat her.

"Open the door, honey! Daddy ain't gonna hurt you! Daddy loves his li'l girl. He just wants to show her how much he loves her."

Yeah right, Tammy thought as defiantly as her fright permitted her to. *By sticking your huge thing in my butt again.*

"C'mon, honey, you know you love daddy too!" He'd begun shaking the door, turning the door knob back and forth.

Tammy squirmed under the comforter, fretting over what to do. This had been going on for three long months now, ever since her mother had gotten that waitressing job.

At first, Tammy had been delighted to have her mother out of her hair in the evenings, but then her father had seemed to 'notice' her. First he'd begun patting her behind when she walked by him and commenting on "How much of a woman" she was fast becoming. Then he'd begun squeezing her buttocks when he got near her.

And then finally, one night he'd simply forced himself on her, entered her room roaring drunk with his pants already down and his penis poking out, and thrown Tammy down on the bed, forced her kicking legs wide and stuck himself deep inside her body. It had hurt like hell and there had been a lot of blood, but he'd persevered, while she'd wept and moaned in pain. Finally, he'd pulled out and ejaculated all over her belly.

"Yeah, that's a good girl," he'd said afterwards. "Now clean up the mess and remember not to tell your mom what I did to you or there'll be dire consequences."

Now the drunken voice rumbled again: "Tammy open up this goddamned door right now or I'm gonna break it down! You hear me, you li'l bitch? What kinda way is this to treat your daddy?"

The door shook with the threat. Tammy didn't doubt that he'd carry out his threat and break down the bedroom door. And then her mother would blame her for provoking him.

Of course she'd told her mother what was going on. But her mother either didn't believe her or didn't care. Halfway through Tammy's explanation about the nightly rapes, she'd silenced the girl with a slap. "Stop lying about your father, girl! You know how hard he works to look after you!"

That had been the end of that. And so for the past three months, 14-year-old Tammy Young had been getting violated at least thrice a week.

She'd wanted to tell someone her problems, but didn't know who to talk to. Everything she'd read online said family's like hers tended to be split up, and she didn't want to be responsible for that. She had it hard enough already. She was a gawky girl, unpopular at school, and she was certain that if she made a fuss about her father's unwelcome nighttime attentions, she'd merely become the subject of additional ridicule. So she'd persevered in her suffering, becoming more and more withdrawn while hoping and praying that her mother would soon lose her waitressing job at the diner and take to staying home again in the evenings.

But so far that didn't seem about to happen.

And for Tammy, things had only gotten worse. Of recent, her father had switched to violating her anus instead of her vagina. That hurt even more than doing it the normal way. Lots of times there was blood in her stool afterwards.

Tammy honestly didn't know how much longer she could go on like this. She'd already begun contemplating suicide. Or murder. But she knew that if she killed her father, her mother would be mad as hell; would denounce everything she said as lies and hand her over to the police without a moment's hesitation. It really looked like she couldn't win.

"Open this frigging door right now, you li'l bitch, or else!" He was screaming at the top of his voice now and pounding hard on the door. The door shook with each impact of his fists. Tammy expected it to splinter inwards at any second.

Feeling miserable, Tammy got out of bed and trudged over to open her bedroom door, considering the miserable fact that her house was situated so far out of town that no one would hear her screams even if she was being killed.

The moment the door opened, her father grabbed her by the neck and slapped her hard. He was drunk as hell, his alcoholic breath raining on her so she felt like throwing up. She didn't though; that would just make him madder. She let him force her back towards the bed. He was huge and hairy and his eyes were bloodshot from all the beer. His pants had been discarded somewhere on the way upstairs to her bedroom and as he stumbled against her, his erection prodded her in the belly.

"How dare you dare keep me waiting outside like that?" he growled at her.

Then he shoved her down onto the bed, rolled her over onto her belly and without any preamble forced himself into her tender behind.

Tammy shrieked with pain and tried to escape, but her father was simply too strong for her to shift him off her. He lay on her like a huge hairy ape, thrusting like he was punishing her disobedience. He didn't speak now, just growled like a beast, while poor Tammy lay there squashed into the mattress with her hands balled into little fists, biting her pillow to keep from screaming.

It was after a while of this that the shadow descended over them. Through her tears and the shredded feeling between her buttocks, Tammy Young suddenly noticed that the light in her bedroom seemed to have dimmed. Then she heard her father shriek with pain, and then she felt him pull out of her anus, and then his weight completely lifted off her body.

She lay there, gasping out her relief that the night's torment was over. Maybe he wanted to come on her breasts like he sometimes did. She lay there with her face still pressed into the pillow, her teeth clamped firmly on its softness, hoping such was the case.

But no, daddy was howling with pain.

"Help me!" he shrieked in a drunken gurgle. "Help me, Tammy!" Mixed in with his terrified yelping was a loud snuffling sound that sounded almost like his recent grunting atop her.

Tammy rolled over to see what was wrong with him.

She was instantly filled with a fresh rush of terror. Something had a hold of her father from behind, and the thing was ripping into his neck with long bloody teeth.

Dragging her father along with it, the creature had moved back out of the light now and the light was in Tammy eyes, so that for those initial seconds after sighting it, all she made out of the thing was that it was black. But slowly, clearer impressions filtered in through her fear. Now she saw that it was a giant human-bat hybrid of some sort, a nightmare monster. Its wings extended from its wrists to its ankles, forming two leathery gray sheets in which it wrapped her father as it killed him. Each wing had five or six long, bony and hinged spines projecting down from the armpit which extended the wing away from the body, and which billowed out like an unfurled umbrella when the arms were spread. The monster smelt very old.

Blood pouring from its mouth, the monster momentarily lifted its head from savaging Tammy's father's neck and stared at her. Its head was a huge wedge of flesh and hair and ears, and its glowing red eyes projected a horrifying hunger at her. With the bat-thing's teeth now withdrawn from her father's throat, jets of blood squirted from the deep punctures they'd made in his flesh and splashed her bedroom wall. There was blood on her bedroom floor too; spreading in a puddle around the monster's clawed feet.

The monster howled as if enraged by all this loss of blood and then sank its teeth back into the dying man's neck and sucked deeply again.

Tammy had sat in bed staring like one petrified, watching the creature's gullet moving, but now she swung into action. She leapt down from the bed and ran for the door.

She almost made it. But just as she reached her bedroom door, the monster bat flung away her father's exsanguinated body and grabbed her instead. It dug its claws deep into her arm and yanked her back towards it.

A few seconds later, Tammy was staring into its horrid red eyes, eyes that glowed with a pitiless, ageless bloodlust. She read her death in its gaze.

She made one last attempt to get away, but it now had a firm grip on both her left shoulder and her head. And then she felt it tugging on her head.

Tammy was aware of her neck stretching painfully and then of a blinding pain in her throat as the creature wrenched her head completely off her shoulders.

CHAPTER 20

The Red Haze Dissolves

Immediately after ripping off the teenaged girl's head, the giant vampire bat clamped its mouth over her neck and sucked her blood deep into itself. At first it had no need to suck hard, the natural pressure from her heart forcing the blood into its mouth. Then the heart stopped working and the monster sucked out the rest of her redness, exerting as strong a suction as it had on her father.

But something was wrong. Yes, it felt delight at exerting its savage force on these two puny human nobodies, delight at slaking its thirst by draining them both; but even as their sweet red elixir of life filled its belly and calmed its raging hunger, the satisfaction the vampire felt seemed to drain from it. Initially, while emptying the man, this shift of feelings had been merely a niggle, but as he drank the headless daughter too, it became something that couldn't be ignored. The monster's belly revolted at its delicious meal. Its head filled with noise and pain and its limbs stiffened and trembled.

Suddenly the vampire was throwing up its meal. Powerless to control its upset stomach, the creature first flung the dead girl's corpse away and then fell to its knees, its mouth spewing jet after jet of redness across the teenager's bed and onto her wall, coating her array of pop posters with crimson wetness.

The vampire heaved and heaved, each additional puking making it weaker. And somewhere in the middle of this physical crisis, it lost the battle to hold itself in its altered shape and, with a sudden compacting of itself, became a man again.

A man who remained in the same kneeling position and who, like the monster he'd been, continued to vomit. Vomit until there was nothing left to throw up anymore.

CHAPTER 21

River

Finally, River managed to get up off his knees.

I need to find a cure for this before it fucking kills me! he growled as he staggered to his feet.

If all his retching had had one positive effect, it had temporarily neutralized his hunger. The way he felt at the moment, River didn't think he'd be able to eat anything for the next year.

He sat on a dry patch of the dead girl's bed and stared at her father's corpse. The bodies and blood didn't upset him; nor did the mess he'd made of the bedroom. He'd hunted human prey before, many times. Killing held a delight for him. Even now, while waiting for his stomach to settle, River felt the afterglow of how he'd killed the pair as a soothing feeling.

He wasn't disgusted by what he'd done to these two people. Rather, he was disgusted at himself for not being able to keep the meal down. His belly was once more empty. And even though his stomach felt numb now, soon he was certain to be hungry again.

If this keeps up, I'm very likely to starve to death before I get cured. And I will get a cure for this.

He made a cold gesture across the room with his fingers, his eyes finally finding the teenager's head wedged in the angle between her wardrobe and study desk. The girl's eyes were shut, her mouth open, with blood from her torn neck staining the desktop. Her body was jammed between the bed and the wall, with only her feet visible.

River smirked at the memory of how easily he'd ripped her apart; at how simple it had been to destroy her. *If being this weak is what being human means, I don't want any part of it.*

But like it or not, a huge weakness came over him then. He tried to resist it, but all that vomiting had really weakened him. The desire to rest was too strong to ignore. So he let himself drop back onto the bed and shut his eyes. He let his thoughts drift, keeping in mind that he mustn't fall asleep now, no matter what. Not with this human mess all around him.

No, I'm not gonna live like this for very long.

A rage filled him then, intense anger at this injustice he was being subjected to. He had a sudden suspicion that Dr. Xerxes knew the humanitis cure and was hiding it from him.

I'll go see that sonofabitch and get the secret from him, if I have to tear it from his screaming throat.

But he calmed himself again. The Vampire Society would expect him to do exactly that—try to break into the BSS clinic. They were certain to have some guards stationed over there now, just waiting for him to make such an attempt.

River laughed. *No, you fools won't get me that easily. And I will find a cure for this ailment and I will be back as one of your leaders.*

After all, a vampire didn't kill a vampire with no justifiable cause. And he'd committed no offence.

I've merely contracted a sickness. Once I'm healed, they'll have nothing against me anymore. They'll all have to apologize to me. And then Max King will surely give me back my position.

With that thought, River remembered that he had no money on him. He scowled. *Well, the dead guy should have some cash at home. I'll have a look through his pockets later. Who knows, this may even be a good place to hide out for a few days.*

***

"Daniel? Tammy? Where are you two?"

River jerked awake. *Shit, I dozed off! Someone's come in. I can't have them alerting the police to my presence here!*

"Daniel! Tammy! Answer me, someone!"

The voice was female. The caller was outside in the corridor and was approaching the bedroom. She'd be here any second now.

"Daniel, honey, where are you and Tammy? Are you two okay?"

River waited. He waited while a fat, hassled-looking woman stopped in the doorway. Waited while she slowly took in the carnage in the room—the blood sprayed everywhere; her husband's half-naked corpse; her daughter's head up on the study desk, with the reading lamp bent over it like a hat; and finally himself sleeping amidst their dead bodies. River waited while her mind processed all this information. It amused him a little, how long it took for her to go from confusion to fright.

"OH, MY GOD, NO! HELP!" she finally screamed when her mind made the terrified connection.

He leapt off the bed at her just as she turned to run, catching her before she'd even taken two steps.

The fat woman seemed to turn to putty in his hands as he pulled her towards him. Weak and shivering with fear, trembling with unsuppressed terror, almost peeing herself when she saw the extended fangs in his mouth.

At first River thought of biting her, of tearing her throat out with his teeth and letting her bleed to death. But tempting and natural as these thoughts was, he decided against it. Instead, he moved both hands to her throat and strangled her.

Once the woman was as dead as her daughter, River flung her corpse on top of her husband's and then returned to the bloodstained bed to rest some more. Strangling the woman, digging his fingers into her fat throat while she fought to get free, had tired him out again.

So he lay in bed and shut his eyes for a second time, certain now that no one else would be disturbing him tonight.

CHAPTER 22

Crystal . . . Sunday

"We don't know where he is and the vamps don't know either," Josie said rather impatiently over breakfast the next morning. Breakfast was lots of toast with butter and jam. Coffee for Josie; milk for Crystal.

"The difference is, they know where to look and we don't," Crystal countered, washing down her latest bite of buttered toast with some milk. "You heard the recording: they've waiting for the boss to do something silly, like butcher an innocent family just 'cos he's thirsty."

"Yeah, like that'll ever happen. Hey, pass the jam!"

Crystal slid the strawberry-jam jar across the table to Josie, watched her scoop some out with her knife and spread it thick over a slice of dark bread. Josie concentrated intently on what she was doing.

It was late on Sunday morning and Crystal felt lazy. Lazy but unable to relax. The warm sunlight streaming in through the windows made her feel like she should be out and about working at something.

"I'm bored," she told Josie.

"Me too. We could clean the house." Mouth full, she gestured around with her slice of toast. "Looks like two sows live in here."

Crystal didn't feel like working. "I'm not *that* bored."

Josie looked away from the disarrayed living room and pointed her toast at Crystal instead. "You're not bored, you're *restless*. We're both restless."

Crystal nodded. Yes, Josie was right. Both of them had initially been scheduled to work shifts this afternoon, but with Haven shut due to all the vampire deaths over there, there was nothing to fill the day with now.

"It's like this," Josie went on, licking a smear of strawberry jam off her lips. "We feel like we should be doing something about the damn vamps—looking for runaway River at least—but at the moment we're frozen where we are. We can't do a thing till the vamps find him."

"Yeah, that's about right," Crystal agreed. "I hate having to rely on those bloodsuckers for anything."

"I love how the vamps are so disorganized right now," Josie said. "Without the fangs they could almost be VEINS."

Crystal finished her glass of milk and nodded. She'd been thinking that too. Ever since the first series of deaths during the assassination attempt on River, the atmosphere in the nightclub had slowly been getting tenser, like a string being tightened. Since River's escape the tension was practically electric. Of course, the tension was only noticeable to those in the know: she and Josie; Tony, Olivia and the security guys; and Annabelle and the three new vampires who'd been drafted to the club yesterday to take over the jobs of those who'd died from the sunlight let in through the broken office window.

How Annabelle Robinson had survived that incident was a mystery to Crystal. She could only surmise that the vampire woman had either been near the corridor entrance at the time and had flung herself outside to safety the moment the office window had shattered, or that she'd had the presence of mind to quickly shut herself in an office closet while the unexpected influx of sunlight reduced her two companions to ash and grease.

At the moment Annabelle was running Haven. Crystal had seen her just once since the incident that had summarily promoted her. She'd looked calm enough, but Crystal was certain the vampire woman was very worried. Worried that what had happened to her predecessor just might happen to her too.

"I wish we had some vampire to stake," she told Josie.

"Yeah," Josie agreed. "It'd be something to do. Here we are, two hot young women in their mid-twenties without a social life 'cos we don't wanna attract any attention to ourselves. Josie wiped her mouth clean and got to her feet. "I'm twenty-six—I should be waking up in

my boyfriend's bed and having him serve me breakfast in bed, not"—
she looked angrily at Crystal—"hanging out with you all the time like
we're codependent on each other and . . . and have to keep screwing
Pete the Security Guy for information."

Crystal got up from the dining table and began to gather the plates
together. "How's he in bed anyway?"

Josie pushed her own chair back and got up to help her. "He's fine,"
she admitted, as she returned the butter and jam back into the fridge.
"He makes me come and all that. But you know what I mean. I'd rather
not do him—he ain't that good-looking—and there's lots of handsome
men out there I could be dating. I curse VEINS every time I have to
turn down some really handsome guy 'cos I don't want the vamps to
get a line on us through him."

Crystal mused on that a bit. Yeah, vampire hunting had really killed
their social lives. Personally, she couldn't remember the last time she'd
had sex without there being some investigative angle involved in it.
Different men, all involved with the nightclub in some way, two of
them vampires even. Everything and anything for the cause; eliminate
the vampire race by all means necessary. The cause was supreme, even
when one was disconnected from the center.

And they'd still had no reply from the VEINS servers to their
question about Max King's identity. Josie had run several checks online
for information about the man, but all she'd come up with was the
usual spiel: rich émigré from Germany in the 70's; owned Kingdom
Liners, a worldwide shipping company; and was a reclusive widower
with a rather trashy daughter. (The daughter was at the Haven club too
now.) There was nothing dirty or intriguing about this old man—other
than the fact that the WV vampire organization had thrown a huge
party welcoming him to the state. But Crystal and Josie were cut off
completely from the folks who might know the real dirt about Max
King.

"You know how I really feel at the moment?" Josie asked while they
did the dishes together, then went on without waiting for a reply, "I
feel like we just got off a sinking ocean liner. Imagine us as the crew of

something disastrous, like the Titanic for instance, without DiCaprio to save our asses. I imagine VEINS as that giant liner that's just sunk, vanished into the depths of the ocean, and we're both in a lifeboat, a group of lifeboats even; but during the night our lifeboat drifted away from all the others and so we're all alone out on the wide expanse of sea with nothing, absolutely nothing at all in sight, and the hot sun overhead, and we're just drifting along aimlessly and hopelessly praying for some random cruise liner to spot us and take us aboard." She nodded as she toweled her hands dry. "Yeah, Crys, that's exactly how I feel."

"I don't think it's that bad," Crystal said. Then she shut up. Josie had exactly stated her own thoughts too. *We have been abandoned,* she agreed in her mind. *We've been put in a position where we can't do anything that might jeopardize the cause, and yet at the same time we're duty-bound to carry on striving.*

She shrugged, dried her own hands and followed Josie out of their kitchen into the living room. "So, what are we doing today?" she asked as Josie picked up the remote control. "Watching TV or watching TV?"

"I wish we had a vampire to stake," Josie said. "Even killing a little teensy-weensy baby one would make me feel so much more human." Then as the TV came alive, she grinned. "Hey, we could sneak into the club tonight and stake Annabelle. Ha ha—that'd really shake up the vampire empire!"

Crystal rolled her eyes. "Not on your life. With the type of surveillance they'll have in there now, we'd just wind up in the club basement donating our blood to the evil vampire cause."

Josie nodded. "Hmm, weird you should mention that."

"Huh?"

"Yeah, about surveillance. Pete was telling me yesterday how they're bringing in more CCTV units: they're installing them in Annabelle's penthouse suite and the corridors. The vamps are getting *really* paranoid, you know."

And we are getting to the end of our tenure in that blood-soaked house of theirs, Crystal thought. *It's getting more dangerous by the day. It's merely a matter of time before someone thinks of installing voice recorders in the stairways and elevator too.*

She smiled at Josie, who'd tuned the TV to Cartoon Network and the Powerpuff Girls.

Then her cellphone rang. She walked over to the coffee table and picked it up.

"It's Jerry," she mouthed to Josie. "Turn the sound down!"

Josie muted the TV. Crystal put the phone on speakerphone. "Hey, man, what's up?"

"Hi, Crys, what're you girls doing today? Is it still panic central over at vampire haven?"

"Yeah, they're all still shitting fear and wondering if they're gonna be the next to go. As for us humans? The club's shut today while they mourn their dead. We're both going out of our minds with boredom."

Jerry laughed. "Us too, and still no word from the VEINS higher-ups. Hey, ladies, Sheila's wondering if maybe you'd like to come over for lunch with us."

Crystal looked over at Josie, then said, "Yeah, that'll be just great."

"We're having steak," Jerry said, then laughed louder. "Steak—get it?"

"Oh, I really wish I had a vampire to stake right now," Josie said after Jerry hung up.

"Me, I wish the vamps would all die and rot and go to hell and burn there forever," Crystal said with deep feeling. "Then you and I wouldn't need to worry about being bitten by them all the time."

CHAPTER 23

River

It was 10 a.m. when River awoke that Sunday morning. With sunshine streaming in through the open bedroom window, he sat up and rubbed his eyes. Slowly, the memory of last night filtered into his mind.

He was still in the bedroom of the house he'd entered last night, with three corpses strewn around him: father, daughter in two pieces, mother with her tongue protruding from her dead face. All three bodies frozen in rigor mortis. The blood on the walls and floor had now dried but the bedroom smelt of death.

To a vampire, death smelt nice. But each moment, nausea threatened to overwhelm him again.

The three bodies intrigued River for a few moments, and he spent the interval before his brain began working properly studying them. His attention was particularly called to the dark bruises his fingers had made around the mother's neck.

But then he lost interest in the dead family. They were nothing, merely the latest in a long stream of victims who'd died to feed his predatory instincts.

He turned his thoughts inward, to his own predicament. He was surprised that he'd slept all through the night without awakening. The first result of this long slumber was that he needed to pee. The second was that he was very hungry now, though the sleep seemed to have shaved the edge off this craving for nourishment.

He got to his feet and walked into the dead girl's bedroom.

Afterwards, he sat on her bed again. He'd already realized that he couldn't remain here for very long. Sooner or later, someone was certain to come looking for the dead people. And where was he anyway?

He got off the bed again, walked over to the doorway and picked up the dead woman's handbag. Rifling through it produced her driver's license. Her name was Helen Young and she lived at No. 24 Birch Hollow Road. The address surprised him. *I'm still in Cheat Lake?* Even though in his wolf state he'd traveled quite a distance, he'd apparently gone in circles: Cheat Lake abutted on Morgantown's east side. From here it would be very easy to return to the Haven club if necessary.

Returning to the nightclub? A tempting proposition viewed one way, but a stupid one once properly considered. All that waited for him at the club was capture and an undignified death.

But at least I know where I am now. He imagined an instinct had made him follow Cheat Road northeast to its end.

He searched through the woman's purse for money, then took out $50 in small bills and her car keys. The problem of transport was solved for the moment; though once the massacre was discovered the car would automatically become useless to him.

He left the daughter's bedroom then and made his way downstairs. He still intended to search her parents' bedroom for more money, and hopefully a gun too, but he was hungry. His stomach's rumbling could no longer be denied.

If blood won't quench my cravings, maybe normal food will.

Almost immediately River stepped into the Young's kitchen he realized he'd been right. Last night, Mrs. Helen Young had bought groceries on her way home from work; these lay now in three shopping bags which she'd not had time to unpack before meeting her bitter end at River's hands. He smelt bread and cheese, and apples and oranges, and a portion of smoked turkey. Those were the smells he recognized anyway. The food smelt fantastic to him, as appealing as blood had just a week ago. He quickly unpacked the bags, loaded the food on a tray, and carried the tray out to the dining room, impatiently stuffing slices of turkey into his mouth as he went.

Wow, I'd forgotten human food was this delicious!

He made a trip back to the kitchen for something to drink. He'd have preferred coffee but couldn't find a coffee maker and the Young family didn't have any instant brands. So he got out a bottle of water from the fridge and took it back with him.

Once back at the dining table, he devoured the food ravenously. He simply couldn't get over how good it all tasted. Even with the many recipes vampire chefs had originated through the years to spice up their undead menu, the fact remained that vampire food consisted primarily of blood; that was all that kept them alive, and what their corrupted digestive systems craved. But now . . .

While eating, he did some thinking too. First of all, his mind scrolled back to his last conversation with Dr. Xerxes. He recalled Xerxes asking him about his recent sexual partners. Was humanitis an STD like AIDS? That would be painfully ironic, River considered. *So all the human race needs to do is to fuck us back to be weak like them? Ridiculous.*

But is Ivy responsible? The possibility annoyed River. He vowed there and then that if the woman was the one who'd infected him with humanitis, once he was fully a vampire again, he would track her down and kill her. He'd kill her slowly and painfully, extending her suffering out over a period of weeks. At the end he'd rip out her heart and eat it raw.

But first of all, I need a cure. The longer I remain like this, the more danger I'm in.

***

When he'd consumed enough for two meals without throwing up, River got up and made his way back upstairs.

He wanted to check on his reflection. Earlier, while peeing, he'd seen it in the bathroom mirror, but, still groggy, hadn't paid any attention to it. He strode along the upper corridor to the master bedroom, then stood before the wife's dressing mirror.

Yeah, I was right, I'm more solid now.

A visible improvement. He could still see through himself, but now his image had begun imposing itself on its surroundings; it no longer looked timid and unwelcome. He wasn't 'half and half' yet, more like a third of the way to solidity.

Xerxes said I'll be fully human when my image is completely solid. At this rate I may last two weeks. Hell no!

But then, the noise of a passing car shifted his thoughts again. He walked over to the bedroom's front window and stared out of it, noting the house was situated twenty yards in from the road, and was surrounded by a neat fence of white pickets. There were no neighboring buildings, just grass and trees.

At the top of the road another car rolled towards the house.

With the drapes open, the sun was scalding hot on River's face, reminding him that he wasn't exactly human yet and threatening a repeat of yesterday's instant sunburn. He stepped back from the window and pulled the drapes shut.

I'd better see if there's a gun anywhere in the house.

He turned around to do just that, but then found himself staring at the mirror. *Hey, if my image in there is getting more substantial, what else is new?*

With that thought in mind, River attempted to transform himself into a wolf. Yesterday, the change had been automatic, a survival reflex when the police had been closing in on him. But now, he found it hard going. By the time he was down on all fours on the bedroom rug and covered in fur, he was all tired out. Thankfully, the transformation back into a man was less draining.

Alright, that's out for the foreseeable future, he thought. *What happens if I get stuck in beast form, or if I wind up only halfway transformed?*

Both were horrible possibilities to consider, and as such ones he didn't entertain for long. Consoling himself with the thought that changing shape might prove easier after sunset, River began ransacking the Young family's house for a gun. But first he returned downstairs to the kitchen for Helen Young's oven mitts. It had just occurred to him that he'd been incredibly foolish so far, leaving fingerprints all over the place.

Shit!—how dumb can you get? This means I'll have to wipe down the entire house before leaving!

The police had his fingerprints, though they'd likely be found to belong to one Troy Vincent, a 60's rockabilly singer who'd supposedly committed suicide by jumping off the New River Gorge bridge, even though his body had never been recovered.

CHAPTER 24

River . . . Departure

River couldn't find a gun in the Young's house. After an hour he quit searching for one, sat down on the bed and tried to compose himself. The time was just approaching noon; the day brighter; the sun much warmer.

Outside, the flow of traffic had increased.

His search hadn't been completely unfruitful. He'd found some money—$300—lying about. That would be useful until he could recover his bank cards.

A quick glance in the dresser mirror showed him the same as earlier, a handsome ghost in his mid-thirties.

He peeled off his clothes. They were bloodstained, though the blood had dried overnight. Still, he would have to discard them. One couldn't walk around wearing the evidence of murder. He'd have to borrow some of the dead man's clothes.

He stepped into the shower and was surprised at how much blood washed off his body once he'd soaped himself.

After toweling himself dry, he felt much better. He picked out clothes from the bedroom closet. The dead man had been larger than himself, but he found some denim pants that almost fit him and a couple of shirts he could wear. His shoes only needed wiping. He packed his soiled clothes into a plastic bag; he'd take them along with him on his departure.

This done, River headed downstairs. Along the way, he peeked into the room containing the dead family. Now that the sun had come up they'd begun to smell a little. He shut the door on the corpses and descended the stairs.

He settled himself in a living room armchair to think.

What do I do now?

Two things were certain. First, that he couldn't remain here for much longer. Someone would surely come looking for the dead people soon; someone unable to get them on the phone; maybe from the parents' workplaces, or the teen daughter's friends. The car outside, the house locked and no response to the doorbell? Next thing would be to call the police.

So, come nightfall I gotta leave this place.

The second certainty was that the Vampire Society was sure to be looking for him now. And they'd keep looking until they found him. River didn't even have his phone with him. He was wary of contacting his friends anyway. At this point he had no idea who would help him and who would sell him out.

In the dog-eat-dog world of the modern bloodsucker, whoever I chose to trust may betray me for their personal advancement. So what's the best course of action now?

He found it hard not to be angry at his abrupt fall from grace. But yet, he also found their betrayal understandable:

A human can't govern vampires; only a vampire can. Right now, all I can do is survive until I find a cure for my disease. Hmm . . . and attack is generally accepted to be the best form of defense. So I'd better . . .

River began making plans. Plans to take the fight to his former brothers and sisters.

He got up and walked into the kitchen. He smiled coldly when he saw the cloves of garlic. Touching the stuff made him feel a little sick but it wasn't anything he couldn't handle.

***

River left the house on Birch Hollow Road at around three in the afternoon, reversing the Young family's red Buick Lucerne back out into the road. Then he parked by the roadside and tried to think of something he might have forgotten. He'd taken money, the garlic, spare clothes and toiletries; quite a long list of stuff; everything he thought he might need. Spare gasoline and a crowbar also.

He'd also taken Mr. Young's cellphone, though lest the cops use it to locate him, he didn't intend using the dead man's phone except in the direst of emergencies.

One thing he'd made certain to do was to pack a lot of human food. He didn't know how long he'd be in hiding for. Also, in case he hadn't done a thorough enough job of wiping down the house and the police found his fingerprints, he wanted to be certain he wouldn't have to go shopping for food. He doubted this though. He'd wiped the house down twice, every single thing he'd touched.

I should be fine, but one never knows.

Finally, he put the Lucerne in gear and drove off. Even though the day had turned chilly, the raw unfiltered autumn daylight felt scalding hot on his body. He feared his skin might blister, but it didn't.

He drove fast.

Morgantown was just eight miles from the state's north border with Pennsylvania, and River now chose to use this fact to his advantage. He turned south off Birch Hollow Road to connect with the Mon-Fayette Expressway (Route 43), then he followed the expressway north across the state line into Pennsylvania.

About a mile into the Keystone State, River turned east off Mon-Fayette onto Gans Road, then drove down towards the town of Springhill. Halfway along this portion of Gans Road, he turned the car off the road and parked it deep in the forest.

Now it was a waiting game until nightfall.

River already had a destination in mind.

***

The sun set at 6:40 p.m. An hour later River drove out of the woods onto Gans Road and headed back down to West Virginia.

However, instead of returning to the state via the Mon-Fayette Expressway, this time he took the eastern Fairchance Road route, which also ran right back into the Mountain State, and in addition, extended all the way down to Cheat Lake. It just saw less traffic. Fairchance Road also had the advantage of leading exactly to where River wanted to go.

Once back in Cheat Lake, River, driving with his eyes peeled, soon found the turnoff he was looking for. It was on the right, about a quarter-mile before one reached the Cheat Lake United Methodist Church.

This side road extended for about a hundred yards, ending at an old two-story building which the vampires had once used for housing visiting dignitaries, long before the Haven club's existence.

The house was surrounded by a low fence with access through two gates. Lots of trees in the compound; half of their leaves dry on the ground. There were no other houses on this lonely lane. Its seclusion was perfect for what River had in mind.

He was relieved to note that the house was in darkness. It had no new occupants then. On the drive over it had occurred to him that after such a long time, and with the Haven club now handling its previous functions, the Vampire Society might have sold this building. But such apparently wasn't the case. The building was still in disuse and waiting for him.

He stopped the car at the front gate, got down and forced the lock with the crowbar. Then he drove the red car inside and parked it in the adjoining garage.

When he stepped through the old building's front entrance, its musty smell of long abandonment was a welcoming scent to him. It spoke to him of safely.

As he offloaded the things he'd brought over from the Young family's house, River smiled coldly to himself. He doubted if any of his vampire colleagues even remembered this place existed. It had been out of use now for over ten years.

Well now I'm ready to go!

CHAPTER 25

Dr. Xerxes . . . Sunday Night

They met up on the roof. Alexia arrived at 9 p.m.

Xerxes had spent most of the day in nervous anticipation. He'd never had a vampire girlfriend before and wasn't exactly certain how to proceed.

You're a man and she's a woman, he'd told himself finally. *Everything else will take care of itself.*

And now she was here.

"It's gonna be quite a windy night," she said once she'd shed her bat form for human shape.

"Yes, it is quite windy," Xerxes agreed. "I trust you had a pleasant flight over?"

She laughed at that. "I never took you for someone so witty. You strike me as the brooding type."

He kissed her cheek, then her lips. Her lips were as cold as a corpse's. But then, in a way that's what she was; long dead and yet not dead at all. Her lips trembled beneath his, he could feel the fire of desire in her. He shifted back slightly so she wouldn't feel his erection. "There's been a whole lot to brood about lately," he said.

"The River situation?" she asked as they walked towards the elevator.

"Yes."

"Oh, I'm sure you'll find an antidote in time."

The elevator descended. Xerxes bent over and kissed her again, she kissed him back fervently, then smiled up at him. She was dressed simply: white tee-shirt, pink cutoff shorts and white slip-on shoes. Her blonde hair looked like the wind had scattered it. Except for her large green eyes, which told tales of timeless evil, she hardly looked like a vampire. And how old was she? Five hundred years old, or more? He wasn't even old enough to be her great-great-great grandson's great-great grandson. But his mind and body responded only to what they saw; a trashily attractive woman of about 30-years-old. Oh, how Xerxes suddenly wanted his time to come when he would shed the chains of age and join the ranks of the eternally youthful. For him, sixty couldn't come quickly enough. He intended to fix his final age at about the same as Alexia's.

"The place looks deserted tonight," she observed as they stepped out of the elevator onto the second floor.

"Sunday night. We've no critical cases at the moment—the few admissions are in the ward downstairs—so everyone's gone home." By now, her eyes were feverish with desire for him, while Xerxes felt as if someone had stuffed a rock into the front his pants. He hoped Mildred wouldn't notice his erection when they walked through her office.

Mildred *did* notice. After politely greeting Alexia, she winked at Xerxes and made a gesture down at his trousers.

"I'll be leaving now, sir, if you don't need me for anything else. I've placed a tray of drinks in your office."

"Yes, thanks, Mildred. You can go home now."

Alexia was already opening his office door. He waited for her to step inside, entered after her, and locked the door.

Alexia turned when she heard the click of the key. "Are you kidnapping me, doctor?"

"Oh, I'd love to kidnap you, but your father would kill me," he replied her in a strangled-sounding voice. He didn't understand how he'd managed to control his desire for this long. Outside in the elevator he'd wanted to grab her and . . .

And then they were in each other's arms for real, kissing each other hungrily. His tongue explored her mouth; her fangs were retracted. Quickly, in a desperate race that both of them would win, they undressed each other. Soon, he had her as naked as he wanted her, naked as the day she'd been born those many Medieval centuries ago; while on his own part, she'd stripped him down to his socks. She was really thin, almost anorexic, with little breasts that didn't require a bra.

They heard the outer door of Mildred's office closing. It shut a little noisily, as if Xerxes's secretary was making a point of her own.

"She's left," Xerxes said in some relief.

"And not a fucking moment too soon."

Alexia knelt then and took Xerxes's penis into her mouth. He experienced a moment's fear, worrying that she might bite him. But no, he quickly felt that her fangs were still retracted and that what she planned for him tonight was pleasure, not pain. And she was really good at it too. In fact almost too good.

"Whoa!" Xerxes said after a few moments of her sucking him, pulling her delicious lips off of his swollen member.

She gazed up at him, her eyes large and glimmering. "What's the matter, baby?"

"I haven't been with a woman in quite a while. Another minute of that and I'm gonna explode in your mouth for sure."

She laughed. "Oh, that's alright. We've got all night, haven't we?"

With that she resumed sucking on him. Xerxes tried to restrain himself from coming but couldn't. In less than a minute he found himself ejaculating down her throat. He stood there trembling, placing a hand on a bookshelf to steady himself, while she drained his balls of semen.

Afterwards, with his penis limp, he cleared off the top of his desk, and laid her on it, with her buttocks at its edge. Then sat in his chair and buried his face between her thighs, her feet up on his shoulders. Her sex wet and juicy, the skin of her thighs cold against his ears.

She almost instantly began coming, holding the edge of his desk and grunting like an animal while bucking her hips in his face. Xerxes was then reminded of Mina's joke of the previous night, about Alexia's "possibly not having been laid in twenty years." He doubted it was that long in reality, but she did have an intense hunger to her that indicated it had been a long time since she'd dated anyone.

"Oh fuck, that was great!" she gushed when he lifted his mouth from her vagina. "You've no idea when was the last time I got eaten." She leaned up on her elbows to look at him and he saw that her fangs had come out now, long and sharp and wet with saliva, as if she'd literally been feeding on her orgasm.

He was hard again now. He stood up and slid himself inside her. She gasped and then her thin body began writhing in delight again, while Xerxes's fingers played with her little breasts.

Xerxes's thrusts slowly grew more and more vigorous, as did Alexia's response to them. It was during her next orgasm that she flailed so hard that one of her hands hit Xerxes's intercom unit and knocked it off his desk.

He winced as it struck the floor. Jerry Foley had just replaced the damned thing. But then he quickly forgot about the intercom unit. Alexia hadn't even noticed that she'd struck it. She was gasping out loud with her eyes closed, her fangs sticking out between her lips in an obvious effort not to bite herself.

"Don't stop!" she groaned when it seemed as if Xerxes was slowing his thrusts. "Don't stop!"

Xerxes picked up the pace of his thrusts again. "Oh God, girl, I'm gonna come again!"

"Yes, come! Come!"

CHAPTER 26

Crystal

Crystal was polishing her collection of anti-vampire weapons, while also listening to the latest transmission from Xerxes's office. Apparently not much was going on tonight at the vampire clinic, just the doctor humping Max King's daughter.

Josie was already asleep; too much wine at lunch with the Foleys, too much beer after dinner. So, Crystal had the living room to herself. She sat cross-legged on the floor with her headphones plugged into Josie's spy-rigged laptop; her vampire-hunting arsenal spread in front of her on the rug.

There were four knives. Each knife was 100% pure silver overlaid on a carbon steel base. Fatal to vampires with the right cut, at the very worst it would leave a wound the bloodsucker would be nursing for months. Crystal didn't really like using knives. Knives meant that one had to get up close and personal with the vamps. Crystal preferred throwing the knives, but she was bad at that. Josie, however, was great with knives, particularly at throwing them. She could hit a vampire in the neck from thirty yards away. Crystal had actually seen her do it.

More hot and heavy fuck noises came from the laptop to her headphones. Xerxes and his vampire slut were really into it: "Oh fuck, that was great! You've no idea when was the last time I got eaten."

Yeah, I'm sure it must've been a hundred years ago that someone last ate that withered hole you call a pussy, bitch. But that's just 'cos you've spent all your waking hours since then draining people of blood!

She controlled her dislike of the vampire woman. The anger served no purpose. She'd have turned the recording app off, or at least let it do its job silently, but there was the offchance of one of the lovers making a statement about the vampires' progress with locating River. So, she let it run, and tried to at the same time concentrate on her task.

Six stakes. Round, two inches thick and a foot and a half long; their tips razor-pointed with steel so that there was no doubt about the impalement. Then the mallet to drive them into the bloodsucker; deceptively lightweight, but its head containing a specially balanced steel core that tripled the applied force.

Lots more gasping into her ears.

There were two vampire stunners or 'wands' as the bloodsuckers referred to them. Just like she disliked using knives, so Crystal also disliked the stunners. The silver-rod weapons (taken from the vamps themselves) were very effective, but carried the same requirement as knives did, that one needed to get really close to one's target to use them.

Much better were the final two weapons in her arsenal: a revolver and taser. Neither of these was for vampires though. Electricity was useless against the undead and silver bullets cost too much, and, unlike with werewolves, where the silver instantly knocked the lycanthrope dead no matter what, bullets tended to go through vampires with little immediate damage. The final result of shooting a vampire with a silver bullet was much like that of dealing them a not-immediately-fatal blow with a silver knife—who wanted to give their opponent a long-term illness when they were fighting for their life?

So the taser and the revolver were for human opponents. While in principle, VEINS had no opposition to killing vampire collaborators, in practice its operators tended to avoid doing so. Human bodies didn't dissolve like vamp corpses did. So the gun would be used only as a last resort, preferably when one could prove a clear-cut case of self-defense.

She picked up the taser and smiled at it fondly. Now this, with its long-range deployment, saw *lots* of use. A taser was a weapon she could really relate to.

"Oh shit! Fuuuuk!" Alexia King gasped out her climax in Crystal's headphones. Crystal winced at the irritating noise.

Then there was the sound of a body moving back and forth, a thump of some kind, a burst of loud static, and then the bug went dead in her ears.

At first she was relieved at no longer having to be a party to Alexia's loud and irritating orgasm, but then she realized what had happened: the lovers had knocked Xerxes's intercom off his desk and in so doing disconnected the bug it contained.

Honestly not bothered in the least by this, but nonetheless motivated by her sense of duty to the cause, Crystal put her taser down again, then looked around for her cellphone. She located it on the couch, found Jerry's number, and dialed.

"Hey, Crys," he said heartily on picking up. "How come you're calling me so late?" She could hear external sounds behind him as if he was driving.

"Emergency. But first of all, thanks to you and Sheila again for lunch."

"Don't mention it. So what's your emergency?"

"The bug in Xerxes's office just cut out."

"Cut out . . . ?"

"He's busy fucking Max King's daughter and they both knocked it off the desk."

Jerry burst out laughing. "They're doing *what?*"

"Trust me, you don't wanna have to listen to it. She sounds like . . . Can you fix it tomorrow?"

"I'll do it tonight. I'm in the area. I'll just drop by and—"

"Hey, be careful, man. Wait till she's gone. There's only four of us left now. We don't wanna lose any more people."

"Don't worry, Crys, I'm a big boy. I'll watch out for danger."

Crystal hung up feeling slightly perplexed. Jerry had sounded strangely excited. She wondered if he had a mistress he'd gone out to see. Or why else would he be out so late tonight anyway?

No answer came to her mind, so she decided to pack her weapons back inside their long leather case and binge watch something on Netflix instead.

CHAPTER 27

Jerry's Plan

Jerry Foley parked his Ford F-150 pickup truck on Ventura Drive, but a good distance from the BSS Clinic. He got out and locked the vehicle, then stepped off the road into the woods and headed for his workplace.

The BSS clinic's communications technician, small and thickset and clad in army-surplus fatigues, made his careful way through the trees. This late at night there wasn't much traffic on the highway here, but one couldn't be too careful. Particularly not when one considered the clinic's clientele. The clinic didn't have any vampire guards, but a vampire might be arriving or departing by air and might notice him.

Considering the consequences of the vampires noticing him made Jerry shiver. He and his wife Sheila had been fighting the undead for six years now and yet neither of them could think of the damn vampires without that fear cropping up inside them. Sheila had admitted as much to him.

"I don't even know why we choose to live this way," she'd said one night, in bed after they'd made love. Sheila Foley was a small and quite nervous woman. "We could live normal lives like everyone else, but instead we're running a crusade against mythical creatures."

"We do it because *we know*," Jerry had replied brusquely, angry with her because her statement had just destroyed his pleasant afterglow mood. "We *know*. We've seen the undead; seen what they do. Seen the harm and destruction they cause if allowed their own way."

"But, baby, we're not stopping them."

He'd wrapped an arm around her and pulled her close. "Don't believe it, honey. The vampires are scared shitless of us. Yeah, they act superior, but they know that, simply because we're human, we'll trump 'em in the end. They can hide and amass all the wealth and power they want, but they know deep in their undead hearts that we're coming for 'em. The bloodsuckers may rest in the daytime but rest assured that they don't rest easy. Their dreams are nightmares of us staking them."

"Jerry, why can't we simply let it alone, let the others fight? Surely we've done our part."

"Because we *know*, Sheila. We know about the vampires, about their horrible darkness that surrounds us. It would be different if we were like everyone else, assuming that nosferatu is merely a myth, something from the warped depths of Stoker's and Le Fanu's minds, watching True Blood and never realizing that TV has merely imitated real life. Sheila, honey, it's impossible to know the truth and live a normal life."

That had been Jerry's argument that night and now, staring at the clinic's walls, he mentally went over it again and decided he was right. He'd find it impossible to live a normal life now—a life that didn't involve trying to eradicate the undead. The undead were in his blood now, and the only way to purge himself of them was to destroy them altogether.

Those were Jerry Foley's thoughts as he crouched facing the walls; his bag of equipment laid to one side. He was thankful for Crystal's call. He'd had no idea the doctor would have a visitor tonight.

His business here was of a different sort, something he'd not mentioned to Crystal and Josie. He'd not even told Sheila what he intended doing. He'd only let her know afterwards.

He smirked. So Xerxes has a girlfriend now?

He waited in moonlight shadows, fifty yards from the clinic's side fence, sitting against a sheltered tree, watching the clinic roof through binoculars for the female vampire's departure.

He remembered the incident that had made the vampires his lifelong enemy; the night he'd come home and found his mother's corpse.

They ripped her to shreds like a she was a side of beef, like something without a shred of value. And they did it for fun. Just for fun.

***

Eight years ago. Jerry was twenty then, still living with his mother. Or rather she was living with him: the house was theirs, the mortgage all paid off before his father's death, he hadn't met Sheila yet and so saw no reason to rent somewhere else to live.

He'd come home from work that night with the definite sense that something bad had happened. There had just been that 'wrongness' about things.

He'd parked his pickup truck and let himself into the house.

"Mom? Mom, where are you?"

Usually the old lady would be in the living room stroking the cat and watching television. Tonight though, she wasn't in there and he knew she'd not yet retired to bed because the lights were on. So maybe she was in the kitchen.

"Mom?"

Yes, she'd been in the kitchen alright, laid out on the kitchen island in naked bits and pieces. Arms, legs . . . her head was in the kitchen sink, staring sightlessly up out of the window at the sky as though she were angry with God for the brutal nature of her passing.

The cat was nowhere to be found.

According to the coroner's report, the jagged nature of the tears in his mother's flesh meant no knives had been used, her body had literally been "Pulled apart by an almost supernatural force."

More puzzling than this though, to Jerry as he stood there that horrible night gaping at his mother's remains and trying not to throw up, was the startling lack of blood anywhere. A murder like this should be a bloodbath, with the floor and walls (not to mention the island the remains lay on) all painted red. But there was hardly any blood in evidence.

But then Jerry had noticed the four puncture marks on his mother's neck. Whoever had decapitated her had clearly held her by the neck and head before wrenching her head off—Jerry could see the dark bruises left by the monster's fingers in the pale truncated flesh.

Jerry had stared at the headless neck, at those four bite marks, two on each side, and felt a sudden terror fill him. He'd felt rage too, of course; intense anger that anyone could hurt his mother like this. But overlying his anger, and so great that it trivialized 20-year-old Jerry Foley's displeasure, he'd felt a sudden primal dread, the like of which he'd never experienced before. Those marks—those were bite marks. Teeth . . . vampires.

Acting without thinking, he'd pulled out his cellphone to call the police, then automatically found himself not making the call yet. Instead, he'd selected his cellphone's camera app and first made a video recording of the state of his mother's corpse. He took his time doing this, and paid particular attention to those puncture marks on her neck. He took several snapshots too. Only when he was satisfied with the evidence he'd collected did he call 911.

Then he'd gone to sit in the living room. He spent the time before the meat wagon arrived pondering what had happened to their cat.

The cops arrived and were even more perplexed than Jerry was. They asked him questions he couldn't answer, then took the body away.

The police never found out what happened to Jerry's mother. Jerry later found out what had happened to his mother, but he never found out what happened to their cat. The cat seemed to have vanished into thin air. He finally decided that the poor creature had been so scared of the vampires that it had relocated out of their domicile – hell, maybe frightened it clear away from their neighborhood.

So Jerry had inherited the house, had gotten married to Sheila and moved his bride into the place. And they'd lived happily ever since.

But every time Jerry went into that damn kitchen . . .

***

Jerry snapped out of his morbid reminiscence. He'd heard the noise of monster wing-beats. Now, staring hard, he noticed a flutter of darkness up in the night sky. He lifted his night-vision binoculars and scanned the sky, nodding when in the center of the green display he saw the monster bat circling and leveling itself out.

He lowered the binoculars. *Now I just need to wait for Doc himself to leave. After all that screwing I don't think he'll have the energy for any work tonight.*

Jerry's assumption proved correct. Six minutes later, the complex gates opened and Dr. Xerxes's silver Infiniti SUV drove out and zoomed off down Ventura Drive. Jerry froze by the trees until the SUV had rolled past him, then he got up, picked up his bag and made his way over to the wall.

He climbed over the wall and dropped down on the other side. There weren't any dogs or armed guards. Part of the BSS's security was the idea that there wasn't any—it was a blood research center and supposedly had nothing to hide.

The only thing to watch out for were the CCTV cameras, which were monitored from the guard house at the front gate. But those were no problem for Jerry. He'd both installed them and maintained them.

Jerry had rigged the CCTVs with a simple gimmick: once he (or rather the signal blocker he was carrying) approached within twenty yards of any of the clinic's CCTV cameras, the main monitoring unit in the surveillance room automatically looped the previous five seconds of video footage fed from that camera until he was safely past it.

At night, with most of the corridors empty, the system was a foolproof one. Besides, Jerry's business tonight was all on the second floor, which, with Dr. Xerxes's departure, was now certain to be empty.

So he made his way across the deserted parking lot with confidence and let himself into the complex's main building by the rear door nearest the staircase. This too was no problem: VEINS provided its members with sets of skeleton keys.

The trick was making it to the staircase unseen. He couldn't use the elevator. There were at least four nurses attending to the human patients in the ground floor ward, and if any of them spotted him here, both his mission and his life would be in jeopardy.

But this too went well. Jerry waited in a short adjoining corridor while a large black nurse walked past with a pair of IV drips, then after a slight pause for the blocker to fiddle with the camera feeds, he dashed across into the stairwell.

Then, heaving with relief, he hurried upstairs. So far so good.

***

Inside the doctor's office, Jerry quickly inserted a new bug into the intercom. The office itself smelt of sex—male and female secretions and lots of sweat. His nose detected a woman's sweet perfume, and also that nasty 'essence of vamp'; a reek possibly inescapable considering the number of vampire conferences held in this room in the past few days.

The vampire's smell was something one acquired a nose for; it was only now, after years hunting the nasty things that Jerry could detect it in the air. And even now he wasn't sure if that wasn't merely self-deceit. Maybe there was nothing to smell except the imagined stench of the bloodsucker's evil souls.

After testing that the new bug was working properly, Jerry resealed the intercom, then placed it back on the floor where he'd found it.

He sniffed the air once, decided that yes, it did smell of vampire, or at least of vampire vagina, and then left to attend to his second task— the real reason he'd dared to visit the clinic tonight.

***

Jerry's second point of call was to one of the second floor laboratories.

Confident that no one knew he was in the building, Jerry walked quickly down the corridor. A number of the labs he passed had large observation windows. The rooms beyond the glass sheets were all dark, their only light coming from the flickering consoles within.

Jerry stopped before a door and tried its handle. It didn't unlock. Smiling, he got out another ring of skeleton keys. He knew this was where Dr. Xerxes was working on his sample of River's blood.

The door clicked open and Jerry slipped into the laboratory. He shut the door behind him and leaving the lights off, flicked on a penlight. He wasn't worried about anyone coming up here for anything, but rather about someone outside, one of the men at the gate, for instance, noticing that the lab lights had come on and deciding to investigate. For this same reason Jerry made certain to keep the penlight aimed at the floor tiles.

Jerry walked between the laboratory tables with their racks of equipment, their computers and monitors, everything static and silent until morning except for the two large refrigeration units at the room's far end which, in the room's darkness, hummed as if with eerie purpose. Each unit had a transparent glass front and its lights were on, illuminating its varied contents, which in most cases turned out to be blood.

Jerry was here to steal the sample of River's blood that Dr. Xerxes was researching on. He didn't know lab technology, but he figured that any specimen tube labelled with a capital 'R' or a 'D.R,' or 'R.D.' must be what he was looking for. If there happened to be more than one, he'd take them all with him. He figured River's blood sample must contain the disease he had, and that once VEINS renewed its connection with himself and the girls, they'd be glad to have a humanitis sample to work on themselves.

"Only thing is not to catch it myself," he said aloud.

The blood sample wasn't in the first fridge. But in the second one Jerry found what he was looking for, a small plastic bottle labelled 'River, Douglas.' The bottle contained about an inch and a half of blood.

Musing on how such a little thing could be so valuable, Jerry stashed it away in a Ziploc bag he'd brought along for the purpose. He had no desire to catch humanitis.

Then it was simply a matter of retracing his steps out of the laboratory, downstairs again, and out of the building.

He had a close shave on the first floor, ducking into hiding just before one of the night nurses stepped out of the nearby private ward. Jerry froze on the stairs and waited, his heart pounding so hard he imagined the young woman must have heard it as she strode past with a tray of medicines in her hands.

Shit! Shit—not now! I didn't come all this way to get caught now. All of a sudden Jerry's confidence vanished like gas in air. He began worrying and sweating, his pulse racing. If he got caught now, with River's blood sample on him, he was as good as dead and just as drained of blood.

But finally, the nurse turned off into a side room and he was free to make his escape.

He slipped out of the side door, locked it, and then, precious blood sample tucked in his pocket, hurried over to the complex wall and clambered over it again.

Jerry didn't feel safe until he arrived home without incident. Then he placed the stolen blood sample in his fridge, undressed, and climbed into bed beside Sheila, who was already fast asleep.

He'd tell her what he'd done tomorrow.

CHAPTER 28

River . . . Monday

Now that he'd decided to take the fight to the vampires, River was no longer in a hurry. He knew Nick Anderson and Mina Cupples would be searching for him, flying nightly patrols over Morgantown and its neighboring communities, and he intended to let them find him.

But not yet. First of all he had preparations to make.

River knew he couldn't take on the Vampire Society single-handed. That would of course be suicidal. What he had in mind was to scare them into leaving him alone. He would set a trap for them, and when they came for him, he would spring it. He hoped the death toll would convince them to just let him be. And afterwards he would vanish. Until he'd found a cure to this stupid humanitis.

But he would be back. Oh yes he would. He'd be back for sure.

And when I return, I'm gonna reclaim everything I've lost. My position, my power and my wealth. So whoever's running Haven now—oh no, Annabelle, you ain't got it made just yet. I'm coming back for what's rightfully mine.

He found it impossible to think otherwise. Annabelle Robinson— he was certain *she* was in charge of the nightclub now Pale Joe was dead—wouldn't be in his rightful place for long. He'd slaved to build the Haven club up, to give it respect and prestige in vampiredom, and if anyone thought he'd let them kick him out in the cold just because . . . well, who ever thought that definitely had another think coming.

No, they're not superior to me. None of them are. I'm better than all of them. I worked for that damn position and it's mine and I will have it back.

***

River spent most of this first day in the old house sealing up its windows. This he accomplished by first shutting them, then drawing crosses on their panes with a can of red paint he found in the basement. The sight of the crosses repulsed him, but he could just about bear their presence; though after treating each window he was forced to quickly shut the door to that room and sit down in the corridor outside to steady himself. This meant it took him very long to finish the task. Once he'd done all the windows he painted additional crosses on every door that led outside the house, including the two loft-access doors on the roof, which were designed to enable flying vampires enter the house from the sky. It was a painstaking job, one which, because of the crosses' weakening effect, seemed to take forever to complete.

With all the rests he took in-between his bursts of painting, River didn't finish his task until six o'clock that evening. The only two entrances he left unsealed were the front and back doors.

But afterwards he was pleased. If the crosses affected him, who was losing his vampire powers, this drastically, they were certain to be a major deterrent to any true vampires who came their way.

Step one was completed then. The work had drained him too much for him to attempt anything else today. He had dinner and fell sound asleep.

CHAPTER 29

The Night News

Monday night.

Nick Anderson and Mina Cupples were over at the BSS clinic.

The problem was simple: someone had stolen River's blood sample. Xerxes was irate, was calling for someone's head, and he wasn't particular whose neck turned up in the guillotine.

"This is a mess," Nick told Mina after they'd been outside for the second time. "The security cams didn't catch a thing and yet—"

"Shush!" Mina silenced him. They were walking through the downstairs waiting room and a 'breaking news' news bulletin had just come up on the television:

"FAMILY OF THREE MURDERED IN APPARENT SATANIC RITUAL"

"Hurry up," Mina told Nick. "Turn that up!"

Nick was already striding over to pick up the remote.

The news anchorman was saying: ". . . This evening, in Morgantown's adjoining community of Cheat Lake, Daniel and Helen Young and their 14-year-old daughter Tamara were discovered butchered in their home at No. 24 Birch Hollow Road." There followed a video of the exterior of the Young family's house; police cars everywhere and covered bodies being wheeled into ambulances; lines of yellow tape, and a small crowd of onlookers.

"Shit—this has to be River's doing."

"Shush."

". . . The police say that from the state of the bodies the murders were apparently carried out last night . . ."

"I told you he'd fuck up sooner or later," Mina whispered.

"And you were right," Nick said in disgust. "This bloodbath . . . it's him, alright. The snobbish sonofabitch never could keep a low profile."

The newsman had little additional information, except to say that the killer had made off with Helen Young's car and was believed to have left Cheat Lake. The murderer's gender was at the present unconfirmed, but viewers in the states of West Virginia, Pennsylvania and Maryland were urged to keep a watch out for a red Buick Lucerne with the license plate 578 D3R . . .

"Come on!" Mina urged Nick. "We'd better get up to Xerxes's office. We'll need to have an emergency conference about this."

CHAPTER 30

Dr. Xerxes & Co.

Arnold Xerxes was still very angry at the theft of his cherished blood sample.

"I don't understand this," he growled at those gathered in his office. "Are you vampires playing a sick game with me or what? Here I am trying to crack this thing before time runs out for us all and . . ."

"I don't think a vampire did this," Nick pointed out quietly.

Xerxes glared at Nick. "Who the fuck else could get into my laboratory without the damn film cameras picking him or her out!?" he stormed. He was too angry to show his normal deference to his vampire associates. "I don't understand how you vamps can sabotage your own efforts."

"Calm down, doctor," Max King said with steel in his voice. "I'm certain Mina and Nick will discover who's responsible."

Xerxes looked at the old man. He felt like saying a whole lot more, but the old man nodded slightly at him and he controlled himself. He sank into his seat simmering. He glanced over at his secretary. Mildred had her head bent over her notepad. Tonight, no one was drinking anything. With Mina and Nick's news about the massacre of the Young family, there was an almost tangible solemnity among the six members of this human/vampire gathering, as though they were mourning the dead people.

"He does have a point, father," Alexia said angrily. "It's got to be one of *us* who stole the blood sample from here. Someone working in cahoots with River."

Max King nodded his old head. "Maybe you're right." He looked seriously at Mina and Nick. "But I have the greatest faith that our security force will be able to discover the truth."

Nick and Mina both nodded quickly. "We're on top of it, sir," Nick said, after which Mina gave Xerxes a pleading look that begged: "Please, just shut up about this, okay?"

Xerxes nodded back at her. He was now back in control of his emotions again. Alexia was sitting beside him, holding his hand. To Xerxes's intense relief, her father didn't seem to mind.

"Don't brood too much on the theft, Xerxes," Max King said. "We'll catch the culprit soon enough. For the moment, let's all focus our mental energies on finding River." He looked at the vampire couple, the muscular man and slightly stout woman. "Nick . . . ?"

Nick cleared his throat. "The police seem to think that River's fled the state. But Mina and I don't think that's the case at all."

"Yeah," Mina seconded, "we believe River is still nearby."

"And why do you suppose this?" Max King asked.

"All his stuff—his driver's license, passport; everything—are still in the clubhouse," Mina explained. "True, he could replace them all, but remember our society is responsible for renewing his identity. He also uses one of our banks and we can turn off the tap anytime we like. But there's a safe in his bedroom with some money in it. And he'll want his ID documents too. They'll get him safely out of the state and possibly out of the country even before we could block them."

"You think he's gonna try to break into the nightclub?" Alexia asked. "That's suicidal."

"Not if he tries it in the daytime," Nick said. "The guards would certainly let him drive in—he hired them all—and the staff would simply assume he'd been occupied with other business over the past two days."

"The club manager is one of our associates, he's in the know," Max King pointed out. "All he'd need do is make a phone call to alert us to River's return. So, no, forget that. It'd be too risky for River to attempt a break-in."

"What if he's working with VEINS?" Xerxes asked. "I know they hate each other but . . ."

Mina immediately shook her head. "Can't happen. VEINS is too decentralized. If *we* can't get a handle on them, how can he? And in such a short time?"

"Wait, everyone," Max King said in an authoritative voice that made them all instantly turn to look at him.

"We're getting sidetracked," he went on. "Let's not spend our time figuring out what River is planning to do to us. Let's instead plan what we're going to do to him." The vampire leader frowned at his two security chiefs. "So yes, you're certain he's nearby—possibly here in this city, even—hiding from us. How do you plan to go about catching him?"

"We intend to send out a series of squads, starting tonight; covering this city and its neighboring towns and communities."

"How are those gonna help if he's in hiding?" Alexia asked.

"Simple," Nick replied. "We got the idea from the newscast about the Young family's murder. River likely thinks he can keep killing with impunity, simply to prove he's not yet lost all his vampire abilities. The needless violence of the deaths proves this."

"You really think he's that stupid?" Alexia asked.

Mina nodded. "River's never been a smart cookie—he's too cocky for that, too sure of himself. He's always thought that he was better than the rest of us. And now, the thought that he's being reduced to a mere human . . ." She locked eyes with Xerxes. "No offence, doc, just saying."

Xerxes waved it off. "None taken. I understand. Go on."

Mina went on: "So, the thought that he's losing the godlike abilities he's cherished for so long is most likely proving too much for him to bear. He's having a mental breakdown. So, yes, he is going to kill some more innocent people. And soon too. Just because he can. And we'll be out there flying," she finished. "Alert for the smell of another bloodbath. These next deaths are certain to be as messy as the Youngs'."

Max King looked pointedly at Xerxes. "What do *you* think, doctor? Do you think it'll work?"

Xerxes nodded. "She's accurately stated my own thoughts, sir. My one reservation to this approach is, with him—River—being in this hypersensitive mental state, there's certain to be a fight when they find him . . . and now, with my blood sample gone, I need him alive so I can take another one."

"We're making allowances for that, doc," Nick said. "Along with the vampire squads, we're also taking a backup van with a human crew. They'll be bringing along a metal casket and also those freezers you developed."

Max King looked confused. "Freezers? What are those?"

"They're actually desiccators, sir," Xerxes explained. "They cover the target's body with a chemical that instantly sucks all the water from it. The weapon is instantly fatal to a human being, but a vampire merely needs an infusion of water to restore oneself back to normal. We call them 'freezers' both because it's easier to pronounce and also because in a sense the target does wind up 'frozen.' " He shrugged. "In this particular case, it's an excellent choice of weapon. River isn't yet fully human, so drying him out shouldn't kill him. But . . ." he made eye contact with both Mina and Nick, "don't spray his head with it. Just in case."

"Yeah, yeah," Alexia heartily agreed. "Just in case, you know, you might want to ask him some questions afterwards."

"So, a nightly aerial posse it is then," her father said. "Alright, good luck with it. We'll break up the meeting now so you two can get started."

That was it then. Nick and Mina left quickly. Mildred quietly withdrew to her office to file her notes.

"Look after my little girl," Max King told Xerxes when it was just the three of them left in the doctor's office. "She's all I have; all I'm living for now." He smiled sadly. "You'd never expect it, but after living for so long, you can actually get bored. Life becomes a habit; one you find hard to break. Yes, occasionally *I do* grow tired of living, but at my age and after all this damned time, what else is there to do? But seeing Alexia happy makes me happy too."

Xerxes nodded. "Yes, sir, I'll do my very best to make her happy." Alexia was pinching his backside while he said this and he fought to keep a straight face. It meant a great deal to Xerxes to be entrusted with this responsibility, as if by dating Alexia King he was protecting the entire vampire race.

He saw the Kings off again.

Up on the rooftop, Alexia whispered throatily into his ear, "Remember, daddy says you're supposed to keep me happy. It's compulsory now—he'll drink your blood if you don't." She laughed at her joke, then added more somberly, "Alright, darling, I'll meet you here tomorrow night. I'd stay now, but dad's more bothered than he looks. Now I'll have to keep him company while he gets drunk on Catholic schoolgirl's blood and retells me the stories of when he and Vlad Dracula were fighting over my mother's virtue."

Giggling, she joined her father at the edge of the roof and moments later, the pair of them soared skyward.

"Oh, what a beautiful sight," Xerxes said as he watched them go. "I really can't wait to be that way too."

Then he returned his mind to the worrisome puzzle of who'd stolen River's blood sample.

CHAPTER 31

River

On waking this Tuesday morning, River put the second phase of his plan into effect. It was time to convert the two-story house into a maze of traps. This was less energy-sapping, but was also more intricate, requiring much attention to detail.

The garlic he'd taken from the Youngs' house came in useful now, as did an axe and chainsaw which he'd discovered in the basement here.

The garlic, being only slightly less repulsive to him than the crosses had been, gave him some trouble with its preparation. The building had lots of electrical appliances, but the power and water had been turned off ages ago. (Last night he'd slept by candlelight; drank rainwater from an old pail.) River discovered that the only way he could grind up the garlic bulbs was by hand, using a ceramic pestle and mortar he found in the kitchen cupboard and which seemed more like an alchemist's tool that something intended for preparing meals. The smell of the garlic almost made him faint, and actually touching its paste blistered his hands. But he persevered until he'd ground it all up. Then, after securing the garlic paste in a jar, he collapsed and passed out on the floor.

When River awoke, it was time to make stakes. This was where both the chainsaw and axe came in useful. For wood, River simply butchered the chairs in the dining room, cutting off all their legs and trimming and shaping them, before finally sharpening one end of each to a deadly point.

141

The thought of actually staking a fellow vampire gave him a feeling of intense sadness. *I seem to be a new species of Van Helsing—the almost-vampire vampire hunter. Not Blade, but close enough.*

Stakes made, the next thing needed was rope. Fortunately, the house had lots of this commodity; mostly used in the past for tying up human victims. As River got a number of coils of rope out of the house basement, lighting his way with a candle, he mused on the reversal inherent in this also—that his old friend's old tools were about to be set against them.

He built his traps carefully, setting them up around the house, and taking careful note of their locations so he didn't step into them himself. They were primitive things, but were certain to work against persons ignorant of their existence.

I've one chance of surviving this. I'd better make it count.

By nightfall, he was through with his preparations. He checked to ensure everything was in its place. It was.

He needed just one more thing: bait.

I'll get that tonight. And tomorrow night the vampires can come for me. And I'll be ready to welcome them.

CHAPTER 32

Crystal . . . That Same Night

"Yeah, she sure is loud, alright," Josie agreed as they listened to the latest broadcast from the bug in Xerxes's offices. "Like she ain't been laid for the past 200 years."

Work at Haven had resumed yesterday. Today, Crystal and Josie had both worked the afternoon shift. They'd gotten in thirty minutes ago and immediately switched on the bug's receiver.

"I still can't believe Jerry stole that blood sample," Crystal said during a relative lull in the transmitted sexual noises, during which the only sounds coming through the headphones were the sound of slurping lips and Xerxes's impassioned grunting.

Josie was eating potato chips. Munching a mouthful, she shook her head. "Too dangerous. I share Sheila's point of view that he's jeopardizing us."

"C'mon, it's a strike against the vamps where it hurts them the most." Just saying this filled Crystal with tremendous excitement. "You heard how desperate they are now to find River; flying everywhere looking for him? And the instructions to take him alive. That's in our favor."

Josie swallowed. "Yeah, I agree that they're scared now. But now they also know someone had access to their offices."

"Girl, they think it's a fellow vampire. Or us—I mean VEINS."

"I still think it's a bad idea," Josie said. "I can practically feel in my bones that something's gonna go wrong. And we've still got no backup."

The loud sex noises had resumed. "Oh, shit, I'm coming!" Xerxes was groaning in both girl's ears.

"You know," Crystal said seriously. "If we're gonna have to keep listening to the two of them doing it each night, I'd suggest we download some porn to watch along with it—muscular dude, skinny chick—that way we don't just have to imagine what's going on."

Josie shook her head. "Better if we just take turns listening, then we won't have to both pollute our ears with their—"

There was a sudden scuffle over the headphones, a loud 'Thump!' and next thing, silence in their ears.

"What just happened?" Josie asked.

Crystal rolled her eyes at the ceiling. "They've knocked the damn intercom down on the floor again and the bug's disconnected again."

Josie began laughing. "Just like last time."

"It's not funny. Now we've gotta send Jerry back in there to adjust it again. And with the vamps on high-alert, I don't think he'll be able to do it tonight. And what if they find River tonight? With the bug out we've no way of knowing."

Josie shrugged. "I don't see why you're so bothered about it. They didn't find him last night, did they?"

"No . . . but . . ."

"So, maybe he's hiding from 'em. Playing cat and mouse. Maybe he ain't as scared or as insane as the vampires think. Maybe he won't kill anyone else, and all the night-flying they're doing will all be for nothing. And besides, they don't plan on killing him anymore anyway. So we've more time to rescue him." She grabbed another handful of potato chips and downed them with coke.

Crystal couldn't think of a reply to Josie's arguments. So instead of replying her, she picked up her cellphone and dialed Jerry. "Hey, it's Crys. Jerry, you're not gonna believe what just happened again . . ."

CHAPTER 33

Bait

One reason River selected Olivia Riley as his target was because the last time he'd seen the Haven club's accountant, she'd just started her period.

He needed blood for vampire bait, and it struck him that a menstruating woman would surely have more of it in her body than one who wasn't. That he could simply have selected a large *man* for that additional plasma volume never occurred to him.

The second reason River selected Olivia was because she lived close to his current hideout. Olivia lived on Donaldson Crescent, just five minutes' drive from the old vampire lodge, and River, who was still driving Helen Young's car, knew the police must surely be on the lookout for the vehicle now. As such, the short distance to Olivia's house was to his advantage.

Now, pulling up to her bungalow at a quarter to eleven p.m., all River had in mind was simply to snatch her and be gone as quickly as possible.

He got out of the car and sneaked over to the house. He'd been here once, several months ago, and remembered the bungalow's layout. Olivia lived alone and her bedroom was at the rear of the house, on his right now. The living room lights were off; the bedroom light was on.

Olivia's house wasn't isolated like the Young family's. She had neighbors left, right and opposite. Her car wasn't visible either; which meant it was parked inside her garage, the rollup door of which was shut. Which gave him an idea.

Deciding it didn't make much difference whether or not she screamed for the neighbors, River simply yanked the kitchen door off its hinges. His fading vampire strength had some advantages. The door made quite a noise coming off, but being on the other side of the building, even if Olivia had heard the noise, she had no way of telling what had made it. She would most likely put it down to some car sound. If she was still awake, that was.

River stepped into the house.

He found Olivia asleep in bed, out cold. It seemed she'd just finished masturbating before going to sleep; a vibrator stood on the nightstand and her bedroom had a faint smell of female sexual secretions.

In one sense River was disappointed: Olivia's period had stopped; she no longer had that heady smell of dripping blood to her. But it was too late to turn back now.

He stepped up to her side, and after a glance to confirm he was in the right house and had the right woman, tapped her on the shoulder to wake her up.

She awoke abruptly, more confused at not being alone than scared.

"Hi, Olivia, how's work at the club going?"

When she recognized him, she opened her mouth to scream for help. Before she got the noise out, River hit her on the side of the head. She slumped back unconscious.

He gagged her, tied her up, and then looked around for her car keys. They were in her handbag.

Once he'd found the keys, he picked Olivia up and carried her through the house and outside into her garage. There, he secured her into the trunk of her brown Toyota Camry, then activated the garage's automatic door.

Once the garage door was up, he reversed Olivia's car out of her driveway into the road, and parked it behind Helen Young's red vehicle. Then he changed cars and drove Helen's car into Olivia's garage and lowered the garage door again. He spent a few minutes wiping his fingerprints off the red car, both inside and out, going over the hood and driver door's frame twice.

Once that was taken care of, River entered Olivia's kitchen and emptied her fridge of all the food it contained. He also found soft drinks and a case of bottled water. And coffee too; he was very particular about needing coffee. He packed the food and coffee into shopping bags and carried them outside and put them in the backseat of Olivia's Camry, then went back in for the case of water.

He made a final trip into the house looking for money, then finding none, he took his time to replace the kitchen door, wedging it in place so it looked undisturbed.

Then he returned to Olivia's car and climbed into the driver's seat.

Olivia hadn't yet woken up: there was no moaning or thumping coming from the trunk. Pleased with this, River started up her car and drove off, back to his vampire lodge hideout.

That was all for tonight. And now he had a new car, one the police weren't looking for.

He arrived at the lodge without incident. By then Olivia was awake again and had begun struggling. River flung her over his shoulder and carried her into the booby-trapped house.

He felt some amusement. Alarm bells were certain to start ringing at Vampire Central once Olivia Riley didn't turn up for work tomorrow.

CHAPTER 34

Crystal . . . Next Morning

All through Wednesday morning Crystal was struck by the idea that something bad was about to happen. There was a toxic feeling in the air.

The first indication she had that something was wrong was Tony's behavior. The day manager looked both distracted and very worried.

Things got even stranger when Annabelle, the new vampire night manager, showed up in the office in the daytime. By now the glass wall in the manager's office had been replaced and Annabelle Robinson remained safe from sunlight on the second floor.

But, Crystal wondered, *there isn't any serious business to handle today. So why isn't she sleeping, like all nasty vamps are supposed to be doing at this hour of the day?*

Then Tony sent Crystal for coffee. This was another weird incident, because Tony Petrelli had a percolator in his office; only this morning he seemed not to remember that fact. Considering the look on her boss's face, Crystal decided not to point out the obvious.

She fetched a pot of coffee for him from the nightclub's kitchen, then called Josie aside into an empty storeroom and told her what she'd noticed.

"Yeah, Annabelle's acting real odd this morning too," Josie agreed. "I asked her twice about the arrangements for Friday night's stag party, and both times she behaved like she hadn't heard me, so I had to keep repeating myself, and when finally she did give me her attention she seemed to think she'd already answered my questions."

"That's just creepy," Crystal said. "I wonder what the hell's up to get her out of her pink coffin while the sun's shining anyway."

"Has to be something big. Hey, have you seen Olivia this morning? We're supposed to be ordering in a monster cake—complete with inbuilt stripper—for the guys on Friday and I need to know who's paying for it."

"Nah, I haven't seen her this morning," Crystal replied without much interest. "Maybe she finally went to see her dentist. You know how she kept saying that her gums were bleeding." Then she looked seriously at Josie. "This is what I was worried about last night when that damn bug disconnected!"

Josie's eyes widened. "You don't think?"

"Yeah, I think the vampires might have found River. That's why they're both so panicky."

"So . . ." Josie looked real focused, "what are we gonna do now?"

Crystal thought for a moment. "Well, we need to know for sure what's going on. There's only two things we can do. First, I'm gonna call Jerry and let him know that repairing that damn bug is now a top priority. He has to get it done latest tonight."

Josie nodded. "Yeah, it's real important now. And second? What's the second thing we gotta do?"

Crystal gave the other girl a wicked leer. "Second is that you'll have to work extra-hard at seducing Pete the Security Guy today."

"Aw shit, Crys, no!"

"Yes, yes—it's imperative that we know what's going on! Something is certain to leak down to Pete, and you'll just have to suck it out of him. Or fuck it out of him if you prefer."

"Aw shit!"

CHAPTER 35

Jerry . . . That Night

Jerry Foley scowled as he made his way along the second-floor corridor to Dr. Xerxes's office. Damn women and their many worries. Crystal had been practically hysterical on the phone while insisting he fix the bug tonight. At one point she'd gotten so irritating that he'd almost told her to go fuck herself. But he'd calmed himself.

So now here he was—communications tech guru to the rescue again. But tonight, he had no need to sneak into the complex after the doctor had gone home. Dr. Xerxes had asked him to install security cameras in his laboratory. Unable or unwilling to use his laboratory with all of Jerry's wires everywhere, Dr. Xerxes had left for home an hour ago. So, Jerry had free run of the second floor tonight.

After fixing the wall brackets for the CCTVs and screwing the units to them, Jerry had left the doctor's lab to go fiddle with the man's intercom again.

If they're gonna keep knocking the intercom down onto the floor, I might have to superglue the bug in place, he thought as he let himself into the doctor's office.

Once again the room smelt of stale vampire. Either the vamps had recently held another conference in here or Dr. Xerxes had been fucking his girlfriend in here again.

The vampire smell was quite strong and made Jerry want to leave quickly. He considered opening the window to let out the stink, but then thought better of it. Someone downstairs might hear or see him do so and he had no business being in the doctor's office tonight.

So he picked the intercom off the desk and with the aid of a flashlight began unscrewing the base cover.

He was engrossed in his task when the office lights suddenly came on. Next, Dr. Xerxes stepped out from behind the long window drapes. With him was a woman; a skinny blonde whose smile revealed long fangs.

Shit—it's a trap! Jerry realized.

Alarmed and frightened, Jerry made to run, but the doctor had quickly reached the office door and was now covering him with a gun. A small pistol—looked like a .22.

"This ain't what it looks like," Jerry said. "Doc, you gotta believe—Yeow!"

The little gun barked like a dog and Jerry felt a sharp pain flood his belly. He looked down at himself. Blood was seeping from a little hole to the right of his belly button.

"See, darling?" the vampire woman said. "We were right, it wasn't one of *us* betraying you."

"Yes, I can see," Dr. Xerxes replied her, with a scary, ruthless look in his eyes that Jerry had never seen in them before. Jerry was still managing to stand, but the pain in his belly seemed to have paralyzed him.

The doctor noticed his confusion and smiled coldly. "I believe I've just given you an appendectomy. It should hurt like hell, but it won't kill you." Then he grabbed Jerry by the throat and slammed his back against the office wall. "You're not as smart as you think, asshole."

Meanwhile, the vampire woman had ripped Jerry's shirt off and was swiping her right hand over the bullet hole and licking his spilling blood off her fingers, a look of rapture on her face. Once she stuck a finger into the bullet hole and Jerry screamed.

"How did you find out?" he gasped at Dr. Xerxes.

"You left your fingerprints all over the fridges. After Mina discovered that, it was merely a case of setting you up to see what else you've been messing with in here." The vampire woman had now begun directly sucking on Jerry's bullet hole. She was kneeling on the floor with her mouth pressed tight to the agonizing puncture and forcing the tip of her tongue into it. He felt her fangs scraping against the skin of his belly.

"For God's sake, make her stop, you bastard!" Jerry gasped.

Dr. Xerxes nodded in amusement. Then he reached down and tugged on the woman's blonde hair till she detached herself from Jerry and stood up. Her lips and cheeks were red with Jerry's blood.

"He's quite sweet," she told the doctor, then meekly sat on the edge of his desk and crossed her thin legs.

Jerry stared at her with intense dislike. She represented everything he despised about her corrupted kind—the dispassionate bloodlust, and the superiority complex, the attitude that humans were merely food. He resisted his urge to spit on her, scared that it might anger her to start sucking at his wound again.

"Alright, enough of these damn games," Dr. Xerxes said in a nasty voice. "Jerry, where is my blood sample? Where's the sample you stole from my lab?"

"I don't have it!" Jerry gasped. "I didn't take it!"

Dr. Xerxes smiled at Jerry, and the chill in his eyes now seemed to freeze Jerry's blood. "Look, asshole, if I have to ask you one more time where that blood sample I took from River is, I'm going to shoot you in the testicles. And the next time I'm going to shoot you in the penis, understand me?"

"I think he means it," the vampire woman said sweetly. "Me, I love sucking bloody penises."

Her words instantly convinced Jerry to confess. "It's in my house," he gasped. "The bottle's in the fridge, in a Ziploc bag hidden behind the pickle jars."

"Thanks for being reasonable," the doctor said. "Now, what your home address?"

Jerry quickly told him.

"Good," Dr. Xerxes said after writing the information down. "You just saved your penis and testicles." Then he shot Jerry in the belly again.

As Jerry sank to the floor, a second trickle of blood dribbling from his belly, Dr. Xerxes told him, "You'd better be telling me the truth, man, or else things are going to get a whole lot worse for you."

A whole lot worse? Jerry Foley couldn't imagine much worse happening to him than his current predicament: two low-caliber slugs lodged in his innards and a female vampire licking her lips while staring at him as if she'd love to resume licking him.

CHAPTER 36

Mina & Nick . . . Vampire Action Countdown

"Alright, Annabelle, you can come with us tonight," Mina said sharply. "Meet us in the air over the nightclub in fifteen minutes. If you're late, we'll leave you behind."

She hung up the phone, then scowled at her boyfriend, who was sitting and watching her pace the living room of their Star City apartment. "Did you hear all that?"

He nodded. "Annabelle is just trying to prove herself capable of handling the Haven club job. River's shoes are huge ones to fill. If, however, she helps us capture him, she'll be recommending herself in a big way, particularly now that Max and Alexia are staying at—"

He fell silent when Mina hushed him. Her phone was ringing again. "It's Xerxes."

"Maybe he wants to come along also," Nick joked.

"Shush, baby!"

Mina listened to Xerxes for a while, with her frown quickly turning into a smile. "Alright, yeah, I got the address. Great job, doc."

She hung up, then told Nick, "The trap worked. They caught Jerry and he confessed. The blood sample's in his house down in Westover. Xerxes wants me to stop by there and pick it up for him. So, you guys go ahead."

Nick nodded, also pleased. "That's one problem solved, at least. So, tonight me and the guys will first fly down to Brookhaven, then up to Cheat Lake and concentrate our search there. We should be in Cheat Lake for at least two hours, so you can easily join up with over there."

He nodded slowly to himself. "Yeah, I'm certain that's where River's holing up."

Mina shook her head. "We need to find him soon, or else Max is gonna think *we're* incompetent and replace *us*." Her voice had become very worried. "Baby, this is the *third* night in a row we'll be flying the skies searching for the bastard."

Nick got up from his chair and walked over to embrace her. "Don't worry, babe. That can't happen. Max is certain to be pleased that we've recovered the blood sample—that's a plus for us. And besides, I've a hunch that we'll locate River's hideout tonight. He made a big mistake by snatching Olivia—it confirms to us that he's in the general area of Cheat Lake."

"I hope Olivia's okay," Mina said.

"She'll be fine," Nick said soothingly. "He's got no reason to harm her. She's just bait to draw us out."

"I hope you're right," Mina said. Then she checked her watch. "Man, we really should get a move on now. According to Annabelle, the human backup crew have been waiting for us at the Haven club for the past hour."

Together, the vampire couple stepped outside onto the balcony of their Star City apartment building, transformed, and took to the air.

The pair of giant bats flew east together for a while, then split apart. The large one flew on towards Easton Mill Road and the Haven nightclub, while its smaller companion turned south towards Westover, heading for Jerry Foley's house.

CHAPTER 37

River

The downstairs living room was lit by three candles placed on the coffee table.

"Please, River, don't do this to me!" Olivia Riley pleaded. "We're friends!"

"I'm sorry, but I have no choice," River apologized as he gagged her again. "Tonight, it's either you or me."

She fought against the gag, snapping at his fingers with her teeth, but he got it firmly back in place. Then he stepped away from her.

He'd tied her down spread-eagled on the living room couch. She still had her nightie on, but it was soaked at the groin, as he'd had her urinate in place, rather than endure the bother of letting her go to the bathroom. The plastic dust sheet was still draped over the couch; the urine was pooled around the bound woman.

Olivia's eyes were wide with fright. She had good reason to be nervous. River had fed her twice during the daytime, but she'd been able to determine from his behavior that this was a one-way trip for her. Her eyes kept going to the coffee table, where River had placed a sharp boning knife.

River sat opposite Olivia and said, "It's kinda strange losing my abilities, you know. I really hate becoming like you again." Then he bent his head and listened. "Yeah, I can hear them already—dark wings up in the night sky, noses sniffing for me and you."

He got up and walked towards one of the windows to part the drapes and peer out at the yard, but then he remembered all the crosses he'd painted on the windows, and quickly drew back.

Tonight, I need to remain strong.

He cocked his head again and listened again. Yes, he heard them, the sound of several sets of massive wings up in the sky, heavy vampire bodies in flight, sniffing for him. Their sound was exceedingly faint; muffled slightly by the noise of the wind but nonetheless discernable.

He turned to Olivia and said, "Well . . . I think it's time I gave your employers and mine something nice to smell." Then he picked up the knife from the coffee table and advanced on her.

She immediately began squirming; flailing, tugging desperately on her restraints.

"Don't use up all your energy now," River coldly informed her, as he bent over her and sliced her nightie open. "You may live longer if you conserve it."

Eyes wide as saucers now, Olivia fought even harder against her bonds.

Then he dug the tip of the knife into the skin under her right breast and cut a deep line down to her waist. Olivia gave off a strangled growl and her body jerked in pain. River cut her again in similar fashion, this time from beneath her left breast to her groin.

As the blood welled forth from the parted skin, he again regretted his degeneration down to the human norm—this red liquid her body was weeping was the elixir of life, and yet it smelt almost nauseating to him now. He was tempted to lick and suck at her wounds, but held back from doing so.

Hell no! I remember what happened the last time!

Olivia Riley was trembling now on the dust sheet, the blood dribbling down over her torso to mingle with her urine. She was staring up at River with pleading eyes.

He ignored her imploring gaze. She was disposable. All humans were.

Time to really get this show on the road.

He placed the knife against Olivia's left wrist, a bit above the rope he'd bound it with, and sliced in deeply. To his satisfaction, the blood spurted out of the cut. He moved to her right wrist and repeated the incision.

There now, this'll definitely let Nick and Mina know where I'm hiding.

As the blood escaped her body in thick streams, Olivia Riley jerked and twitched and bit her tongue, making additional blood dribble from her gagged mouth. The blood poured out of her wrists onto the dust sheet and onto the floor, seeping into the dark carpet.

River left Olivia bleeding to death in the living room and went outside.

Out there, he sat on the warm hood of the dying woman's car and stared up at the sky, watching and waiting.

Anticipation filled him, an expectation at once both thrilling and dreadful. It would be soon now. They'd certainly be here very soon. Olivia's blood would summon them to him, like moths unable to resist a candle flame.

CHAPTER 38

Jerry

"You shouldn't have done it," Dr. Xerxes informed Jerry.

"Look, doc, I'm sorry. I won't do it again."

"Of course you won't," the vampire woman—whom Jerry now knew was Alexia King—agreed. "You'll be in no condition to ever offend us again."

Intense fear filled Jerry at her words. And the way she kept staring at him . . . as if she couldn't wait to sink her fangs into his throat.

"Please, doc! I'll—" he managed to say before the pain from the twin bullet holes in his belly sucked the breath from his lungs and left him gasping in agony again. Along with the agony, his vision began flickering in and out, as if he'd soon pass out.

Jerry was now very worried about his wife. *Dammit, I shouldn't have told these bastards where the blood sample was. I should have bluffed them. If they hurt Sheila in any way, I'll never forgive myself. Shit!*

The office door opened then and Mina Cupples walked in. Mina had a broad smile on her face and seeing that smile, Jerry's heart sank.

Oh no!

"Did you get it?" Dr. Xerxes asked her.

"Sure I got it." Mina produced the small Ziploc bag from the breast pocket of her combat jacket. "It was exactly where you said it would be." She handed the bag to Dr. Xerxes, then turned to stare at Jerry. Jerry felt her eyes rake him like knives.

"It's a shame, all that good blood going to waste," Mina said.

"Not for long, it isn't," Alexia said, making both vampire women titter loudly.

Xerxes was examining the small bottle in the Ziploc bag. "Yes, this is it," he said finally with a deep sigh of relief. Then he looked at Mina. "What about his wife? What did you do with her? You know she had to be a member of VEINS too."

Mina licked her lips. "Oh, his wife was delicious. And afterwards, I redecorated their kitchen with pieces of her body. The cops will have quite a puzzle figuring this one out too."

"NOOOOO!" Jerry howled on hearing this. The effort of screaming instantly restarted the pain from his gunshot wounds and he curled up in a fetal ball, rolling across the floor of the doctor's office, unable to even breathe, with his mind threatening to collapse from the horrible revelation that his wife had just died in exactly the same manner as his mother did eight years ago.

Oh, my God! Is Mina the same vampire that killed mom? The horrible images of his mother's death—her old body ripped apart in that same kitchen, with her severed head in the kitchen sink—filled Jerry Foley's mind. *Oh, my God—so this bitch killed my mom too!*

"Look, guys," Mina said, "I gotta hurry now and catch up with Nick and the posse. They'll be waiting for me in the air over Cheat Lake."

"Yes, certainly," Xerxes said. "Thanks for bringing me the sample first."

"Anytime, doc," Mina said airily and departed.

Once she was gone, Alexia pointed down at Jerry. "Alright, now can I have him? Before he bleeds to death on us?"

"He won't bleed to death for a while yet," Xerxes corrected her. "And your father might want to question him a little. He may have allies, he can tell us about them."

At this statement from the doctor, Jerry felt some hope. *If they don't kill me, Crystal and Josie can still spring me from here.* The intense pain he felt because of Sheila's death made him want to shriek out again, but remembering what had happened the last time he'd loudly expressed his feelings, he managed to keep the agonized noise from exiting his mouth. *And this time, I ain't gonna make the mistake of telling these vampire assholes anything about the girls. Not even if they do shoot me in the dick to make me talk. And once I'm out of here, I'm coming back to stake that mad bitch Mina Cupples for killing my mother and my wife!*

But Alexia King's next words quashed Jerry's weak hopes of escape and vengeful resurgence, as easily as if his hopes had been a caterpillar that had wandered unawares beneath one of the high-heeled shoes she had on.

"Baby, he's a member of VEINS," she said. "They generally don't know any other VEINS members."

Dr. Xerxes scratched his chin. "Well, honey, there is *that* to consider . . ."

"So interviewing him will just be a waste of time," Alexia finished triumphantly, clearly feeling she'd achieved her aim of convincing her lover. "And because that's the case, I'm going to drink him right now."

"No!" Jerry managed to gasp.

"Alright then," Xerxes agreed after a cold glance at Jerry. "But I'll tell your father that you insisted."

"Whatever, baby." And then she was advancing on Jerry with glowing eyes and gleaming fangs, while he scuttled back across the floor to get away from her, with one hand pressed to his bleeding belly, which now felt as if hot knives were slicing inside it.

"Stay away from me!" Jerry gasped, sensing that the most intense horrors of his life were about being realized. Everything he'd ever fought against now seemed about to gang up on him.

"Alright, let's bite!" the vampire woman said with glee, and then she leapt on him and sank her fangs deep into the side of his neck.

Jerry did try to throw her off, but despite her anorexic appearance she was so much stronger than him; her fingers felt like iron nails pegging him down. And soon he felt himself draining away down her throat. Jerry's eyes kept widening with horror, till they felt as if they'd pop right out of his face.

"I'm off to replace the blood sample in the lab fridge before it gets spoilt," Dr. Xerxes called.

Alexia jerked her fangs out of Jerry's neck to brightly reply, "Alright, baby, don't worry 'bout me," then sank them right back in again.

"And, yes, remember to tear his head off when your belly's full, honey," Dr. Xerxes's voice came floating through the gap in the closing office doorway. "We don't want him coming back to life and joining us. There's already enough bloodsuckers in the world as it is."

"NOOOOO!" Jerry Foley groaned, his legs kicking weakly as the life trickled out of him and down Alexia's thirsty throat. "NOOOOO!"

CHAPTER 39

Crystal

Jerry should have called by now to let me know the bug's been fixed, Crystal thought.

Crystal was home alone. Josie was next door in the club with Pete the Security Guy, who today had the late shift.

Crystal was getting very worried. She was sitting on the couch watching an infomercial about some kind of food dehydrator a prominent chef was promoting, praying the phone would ring and lay her worst fears to rest. She flipped the channel. A *Jerry Springer* rerun was playing.

What the hell is keeping him?

A sense of caution prevented her from calling him for an update. If something had gone wrong with Jerry's mission, phoning him would be as good as giving herself away.

So, she waited, her insides knotting with worry as each second ticked away.

CHAPTER 40

Rulers of the Night Air

Once the giant female bat had joined them in their air, the vampires, four in number now—two male, two female—circled swiftly through the night. The lead creature, the huge male that was called Nick Anderson, had caught the scent of blood on the wind, and was leading the other three to investigate. Could this be River?

The vampires formed an ugly group, the only thing attractive about them being the power they wielded as rulers of the night air. They flew, unobserved by man, their very existence unsuspected by man. They flew, glorying in their evil abilities, flapping their immense wings with complete disdain for the puny human creatures bound by gravity to the world beneath them. Indeed, in this exalted demonic form, each of these night creatures felt the desire to descend like lightning, to shatter the windows of a house and sink their gleaming teeth into a shrieking, unwelcoming throat, to suck the red juice of lifeblood out from that body and leave it trembling in the throes of terrified demise.

But not tonight. Now, following the leader, the vampires controlled themselves. There would always be human cattle to bleed. Bloodlust was eternal, but tonight's mission was a thing they could neither postpone nor ignore.

Spilled blood called to them. They smelt it now—its olfactory shriek in their nostrils all the louder and more potent because the blood they smelt was the blood of someone they knew. And it was less than a mile away too.

Olivia Riley's death blood sang to them like a siren.

Finally, the vampires saw their destination right ahead of them, a building several of them knew from the past; a place long forgotten.

And down there too, they could smell their target, the dangerous one named Douglas River.

The vampires circled in the frigid air, preparing to descend and strike.

CHAPTER 41

Crystal

They were at it again on *The Jerry Springer Show*: two overweight young women hair-pulling and calling each other names, with the bone of contention being one woman's boyfriend. Then the guards came out and pulled them apart, while the crowd howled "Jerry! Jerry!"

Crystal's cellphone beeped a message alert. Thinking it must be Jerry Foley, she quickly picked it up. Instead, she saw that it was Josie.

Josie's message read: *EMERGENCY!!! Pack ur hunting gr; gotta muv rt now. Be hm in 5.*

'Hunting gr' meant they were going on a vampire hunt.

Have they found River, or is it Jerry we need to save?

Either way, this was a chance for some action and both she and Josie had been biting at the bit for action for a week now.

Crystal instantly forgot about *The Jerry Springer Show*. She leapt to her feet and raced into her bedroom and began dressing. Black catsuit, sleeveless black jacket with lots of concealed pockets, black leather belt, black sneakers, and a black ski-mask (though for the time being she kept this in a jacket pocket).

Then she got out her leather bag of weapons and began distributing them around her person. Her knives vanished into hidden sheaths in the belly of her jacket, and her wand and taser went into side pockets; her revolver slid into a concealed holster. Examining herself in the mirror afterwards, she looked like she wasn't carrying anything at all, except maybe the penlight in her left breast pocket. The steel-tipped stakes remained in their bag.

Last of all she slipped on black gloves. Now she was ready. All that remained was for Josie to turn up. Crystal returned to the living room, switched the television off and began doing breathing exercises to calm herself and focus her energy. It was hard to relax and concentrate.

Then she heard the front door open and slam and Josie ran into the living room. She nodded on seeing that Crystal was fully dressed.

"What's the emergency?" Crystal asked.

"The vamps have located River," Josie said, hurrying past Crystal towards her own bedroom. "They're on their way to hit him now."

"Huh?" Crystal got up and followed her into her bedroom. Josie was already throwing her clothes down onto the bed and pulling out a black catsuit and jacket similar to Crystal's from her wardrobe.

"How'd you find that out?" Crystal asked while Josie pulled on the catsuit.

"Pete told me." She slipped her legs and arms into the black garment, zipped it up and then sat down on the bed. She dressed with efficiency, with no wasted motions whatsoever. She grabbed her black sneakers and began pulling them on. "We'd just gotten through fucking in the surveillance room when a call came through for Pete. It was one of the guys in the vampire's backup van, telling Pete that Nick and Mina had located the missing package up at Cheat Lake and that they were just leaving to pick it up." Josie smirked. "Pete asked the guy where they'd found it, and the guy replied that it was at the old company house at the turnoff. Of course, I didn't let on that I had the slightest idea what that meant. But when the guy broke the connection, I asked Pete what was going on. He clearly didn't suspect a thing, 'cos he immediately replied, 'Oh, it's River—you know he's been missing for almost a week now? Well, Annabelle just found him. Boss has been on a drunken jag, doesn't remember who he is anymore, blah blah . . .' " She grinned. "So then, acting all surprised, I asked Pete where River had been holing up, and Pete gave me the exact description of the place. It's some disused building off Fairchance Road as you enter Cheat Lake from the north. Apparently easy as pie to find."

Josie loaded up her own weapons into her jacket, the main difference between her own arsenal and Crystal's being that she had more knives. "So I acted dumb like it all meant nothing to me, told Pete that I needed to pee, but that I'd see him later tonight, and that's when I sent you that text."

"Cool," Crystal said, feeling a rush of adrenalin surge through her at this unexpected breakthrough. She checked her watch. "We need to rush. Everyone's got a fifteen-minute head start on us."

"Yeah," Josie agreed, tucking her own ski-mask into her belt, slipping on her black gloves, and picking up her own bag of stakes. "We'd better hurry out there and join in the fun. We definitely don't want the vampire party to start without us, do we?"

"Hell no, we don't," Crystal agreed. "Hey, do I have the bike keys or do you?"

"You've got 'em."

"O-kay."

They left the bedroom and hurried through the house, making one final stop to retrieve a pack of hypodermic tranquilizers from the fridge. One injection of those and it was goodnight, baby.

Three minutes later the girls sped off from the house on their souped-up Kawasaki Ninja motorbike.

CHAPTER 42

Vampires

"The sonofabitch has sealed the building off," Nick said, regarding the old house that used to serve as a vampire hospitality hangout with disgust and more than a little dread. "All those damn crosses everywhere are giving me a headache."

"Maybe they're not *everywhere*," Mina countered. "There's always a way in. We just need to find it."

"Then let's look for it," Annabelle said impatiently. "The longer we wait out here, the more time we give him to scheme against us."

"Be patient," Nick told the woman. "We'll wait for Marcus to return from scouting the rear of the house."

"The front door seems clean of crosses," Annabelle insisted.

"Yes, it does," Mina agreed. "He needs a way to get in and out himself; remember he isn't completely human yet."

"It's a trap," Nick said.

Marcus, the fourth member of the posse, returned then. He was a big, dark man, almost as large and muscular as Nick Anderson. "One of the rear doors is also clear for entry," he informed them. Then he frowned. "Nick, this whole thing stinks of a trap. He wants us to come inside the house, but only through these two entrances."

"Don't be overly suspicious or give River too much credit for intelligence," Annabelle said mockingly. "He's just a playboy who got lucky. He may merely have sealed off the windows to prevent us jumping him."

Mina scowled at her suggestion.

"Maybe so," Marcus said, "but caution never killed anyone."

Nick nodded. "Whatever—we're going in anyway. He's in there and we're getting him out of there." He hefted the freezer gun, a weapon like a child's water gun—with a bubble-tank on top—but made of stainless steel.

"He's bled Olivia to death already," Mina said. "Just to attract us here."

"Sonofabitch," Annabelle spat. "That in itself is sufficient of a crime to execute him for." Unlike the others, who had on military clothing, the Haven club's new night manager was dressed casually in denim, her pale hair clipped back. "Let's head inside and get him."

"You're looking to get yourself killed," Mina warned her. "Let's figure this out first."

***

The four vampires had landed within the old building's grounds and were standing beside Olivia's car. The smell of her spilled blood filled their nostrils. They had no doubt that she was both inside the brick building and that she was dead. They could also smell River in there, something unpleasant stuck between life and undeath.

The human backup van was on its way. After their arrival, the vampires had phoned to tell them where they were, so their associates could just drive in.

The crosses painted on the windows created a natural dread in the vampires. But in this case action was both imperative and impossible to avoid.

"Alright," Nick said, after they'd bounced ideas around for a few minutes. "We all go in. Less chance of him jumping us that way."

"Finally," Annabelle smirked.

"Both front and back entrances?" Marcus asked.

Mina shook her head. "No, just the front way. He may have left two entrances open specifically to make us split up."

"I really don't see what difference it makes if we split up or not," Annabelle said. "There's four of us and only one of him."

Nick smiled coldly at that. "She's right, guys. No matter what he's got set up in there, we've the advantage of numbers." He waved the freeze-gun at them. "We head in en-masse, cool him off, bring him out and dump him in the coffin and call it a night."

"Can we please get a move on?" Annabelle insisted. "I've got some work to handle back at the club. We've been standing out here planning for over ten minutes now."

Nick's lips tightened. "Alright, we go in. Everyone watch one another's backs. Remember, we try to catch him by hand and freeze his ass; our knives are only to be used as a last resort." He turned to the other man. "Marcus, you're in front. Be careful where you step once you're through the door in case he's rigged up some trip wires. The rest of us'll follow your lead."

The big man nodded. "Gotcha, boss."

"Alright, I'll come in second. Mina you're third, Anna's last. No, Anna, don't you dare roll your damn eyes at me—you're so impatient to prove yourself, you'll likely get us all staked by mistake."

Annabelle frowned. "Okay."

"Good," Nick said. "Okay, Marcus, let's knock at River's front door."

***

Marcus slowly pushed the front door open and stepped inside. After a quick look around the foyer, he called back to Nick, "Looks clean in here."

The others quickly joined him inside. Several lit candles sat on the one-time reception desk, their flames swaying now from the breeze coming through the open door. More candles burnt halfway up the wooden stairway positioned directly opposite the front entrance. The vampires could see in darkness, but River's night-vision seemed to have already diminished.

"What now?" Mina whispered to Nick.

"We follow our noses, I guess," he whispered back, pointing to the open living room door. "Let's go see what he did to Olivia."

Behind them, outside in the front yard, the black backup van was just pulling into the compound. Nick waved silently at the two men in the front of the vehicle, then turned back to the others. "Alright, everyone's here, let's do this."

Annabelle however, had walked forward to the foot of the stairs.

"Come back, Anna!" Mina hissed at her.

"Hey, asshole!" Annabelle yelled up the staircase. "We know you're in here somewhere. You can run but you can't hide from us!"

Mina rolled her eyes. "What the hell is wrong with her?"

"Overzealousness," Nick replied.

Annabelle returned to join them, the devil-may-care expression in her eyes daring them to question her actions. Then, halfway back to the foyer, she turned and looked into the downstairs living room, her eyes widening as she did: "Oh, my God!"

The other three vampires hurried forward and also peered into the living room.

"Shit, Olivia!" Annabelle gasped, running over to the club accountant's corpse. In her short time at the nightclub she and Olivia had become very good friends.

Possibly because she'd not been bleeding to death fast enough for his liking, River had finally slit Olivia Riley's throat open from ear to ear, so that now her head wobbled half off her shoulders. Her body lay in the pool of its blood on the couch.

"I'm gonna kill River for this," Annabelle growled.

"No you won't, girl," Nick said quietly. "Except if you wanna kiss your cushy new job goodbye. Our orders are to take him alive. Don't you dare forget that. If you kill him, none of us'll cover for you."

Annabelle scowled at him, but said nothing.

"This damn living room is full of ropes," Marcus noted. "I'd suggest we don't touch anything."

"River is hiding upstairs," Mina said.

"Let's go find him," Annabelle said. "If I spend any more time staring at Olivia's corpse, I'm gonna start screaming the house down."

Nick nodded. "Marcus, you're in front again."

Marcus in the lead, they headed out of the living room.

Marcus had taken just one step out of the living room, when the axe came swinging at him.

"Hey, guys, looking for me?" a familiar voice called from out in the foyer.

Marcus tried to duck, but was too late. The axe swept his head cleanly off his shoulders.

Marcus's severed head flew back into the living room. His body crumpled in the doorway; drenched in the dark blood squirting from its neck. The vampires saw the discarded axe hit the ground and heard their quarry's footsteps ascending the stairs to the second floor.

"River!" Nick growled, bending over Marcus's body, which had already begun to disintegrate.

"Shit," Annabelle growled, her voice filled with both anger and fear, "I'm gonna kill that bastard!"

Leaping over Marcus's crumbing corpse, she ran down the short hallway to the staircase and then charged up it, yelling, "I'm coming for you, River!"

Mina yelled, "Wait!" and hurried after Annabelle. She was just in time to see Annabelle reach the top of the stairs and see her foot snag on a tripwire—a rope she'd ignored in her haste. While Annabelle stood there trying to regain her balance, a bucket upended over her head. Mina instantly caught the smell of garlic. Next, Annabelle Robinson screamed in pain and simultaneously her head exploded, bucket and all, splattering the walls of the staircase. Annabelle's headless body fell backward, almost in slow-motion and crashed to a halt at the bottom of the stairs.

"Shit!" Mina said.

Nick had stepped out of the living room to join Mina. "At least she's cleared the way up there for us," he said angrily. "Let's get up there and get that bastard."

Mina pointed out of the half-open front entrance. "Shouldn't we summon the backup crew to assist us?"

Nick shook his head fiercely. "No. He's just one man, and we're two vampires. C'mon, baby, let's show River what we're made of."

Mina smiled coldly. "I like it when you put it that way."

They hurried to the stairs, ignoring Annabelle's body, which had also begun decomposing.

CHAPTER 43

Crystal & Josie

Josie cut the motorbike's engine at the head of the turnoff and let the bike freewheel silently down the secluded lane. This tactic worked until about halfway down the lane, where the slope of the road elevated again. The bike rolled to a halt.

The girls got off it, hid it amidst the roadside brush, and then carrying their bags of stakes, walked the rest of the way to their destination. They'd caught up with the vampire's backup van a mile back but had then dropped behind it again so the vehicle's drivers wouldn't suspect they were being tailed.

"Creepy place," Crystal said as they approached the building's low wall. The black van they'd been following was parked beside the house, with both of its front doors open. Crystal expected that there'd be two men inside the van. "No sign of the vamps outside," she noted. "Looks like the action's already started."

"Alright, ski mask time," Josie said, slipping hers on over her head.

Crystal followed suit. Both young women now looked like ninjas. Following Josie's lead, Crystal slid four stakes into a fabric quiver designed into the rear of her jacket and clipped her mallet to her belt. Josie slid her small pack of hypodermic syringes into her pants' pocket. They both pulled out their tasers.

"I'll take the left creep, you handle the one on the right," Crystal directed.

With that settled, they clambered over the short wall and, under cover of the night, snuck towards the parked black van. They were both careful not to make any noise crunching the dry autumn leaves underfoot. A giant oak tree stood beside the van, its massive boughs extending out over the van and reaching the house's upper windows. The girls paused for a moment behind the tree to ensure that no vampires were peeking at them from the house who could alert the men in the van to their presence, then, once satisfied that they were still unseen, broke for the van. Crystal crept along the left side of the vehicle, Josie the right side. Both young women arrived at its front doors at the same time.

"Hi, guys, fancy some fun?" they asked simultaneously.

Before the two beefy young men in the van could respond, or even work out where the two 'ninjas' had appeared from, both had been tased. The girls held the tasers to the men's necks for five seconds. Both slumped in their seats, eyes rolling, out of contention for at least the next ten minutes.

"Alright fix 'em," Crystal whispered, climbing in over the van driver's limp body. "I wanna quickly check what they've got in the back."

Josie already had a hypodermic out and was slipping its needle into the arm of the man she'd incapacitated. "What do you want back there? The vamps are in the house, not inside that damn coffin. Hey—we gotta hurry!"

"I wanna see if they've any more of those freezer guns that Doc mentioned stashed back here," she replied, sitting on the twitching man's lap and shining her penlight left and right. "Nah, they don't."

Josie hurried round to Crystal's side of the van and pulled her out of the way. "Let me fix this one too."

Crystal smiled as Josie efficiently injected the driver with the drug mix. This would teach the jerks not to collaborate with the undead. The drugs in the hypodermic syringe would knock the two men out for the next six hours at least. And after that, they'd have vivid hallucinations for the next two weeks. By the time the drug's effects wore off both men would hardly remember their own names. They'd also be useless to the vampires. This was the standard VEINS way of dealing with vamp collaborators.

"Alright, I'm finished," Josie said, discarding the syringe.

Crystal removed the van's keys from the ignition and slipped them into her breast pocket. "Alright, girl, let's get inside the house."

They hurried across the yard and into the building's front door.

CHAPTER 44

River

Two dead! River thought coldly. *That leaves just Nick and Mina. Then afterwards, I'll dispose of the two beefcakes out in the van and use it to make my getaway. I'll drive over to the club, pick up some stuff, and head out of the state, daring them to follow me!*

Now, chainsaw in hand, he waited in the first bedroom on the left as one ascended the stairs. He stood with his ear pressed to the door, listening. He could hear his pursuers silently climbing, impatient to capture him and yet wary of the snares he'd prepared for them.

River was a bit disappointed on that score. He'd set up a trap in the downstairs living room. Had any of the vampires attempted to move Olivia's head, a stake would have shot out at that person from the couch. Disposing of Nick Anderson that way would have been a major coup. But it hadn't worked.

Still, watching Annabelle's head blow up like that was worth it. *Did the silly bitch really imagine she could fill my shoes?*

The two vampires had now paused on the landing. He imagined them wondering whether he was hiding in the rooms on the left or on the right of the upper hallway. This was one beautiful thing about his making such a mess of Olivia downstairs: the scent of her blood would keep drawing the vampire's advanced sense of smell towards it, distracting them from determining his own location. Now they were reliant on guesswork to find him.

Silent though they were, he heard them proceeding away from him, towards the farther bedrooms. They had six rooms to search up here:

three rooms on that side, two on this; and then there was the upper living room opposite this bedroom he was hiding in.

He heard the slight creak of one door, then of another, then of a third. He felt some more disappointment; he'd had another garlic trap rigged on the second door, but apparently Nick and Mina hadn't triggered it.

Next is this door. He rehearsed his motions again in his mind: *Once the door swings open, I pull the chainsaw cord and charge at Nick. Nick is certain to be in the lead. I'll aim for the bastard's head. Once he's dead, Mina will be easier to tackle. Granted she knows martial arts and I don't, but . . .*

The door clicked and then swung open. Nick Anderson's huge silhouette filled the doorway. The man was holding a bulky-looking gun, some kind of weapon that River had never seen before.

Nick saw River. "Mina, he's in here!"

Go! River pulled the chainsaw's starter cord. It almost sputtered to life, but then died on him. He saw Nick aiming the weird gun at him, realized he had no idea what its effect would be, and realized too that if the vampires caged him in this small room, he'd be in a difficult spot. So he did the only thing that came to mind: he flung the chainsaw at Nick. Nick got a shot off, but he was busy dodging the flying chainsaw and so whatever the gun had fired hit the ceiling. Before Nick could recover himself, River had charged into him and knocked him across the corridor and into the upstairs living room. As the two men went flying, Nick both dropped his gun and hit Mina, who'd been hurrying over to his side, knocking her back down the hallway.

Then River and Nick were rolling around on the living room floor, flinging punches at each other and trying to strangle one another; both men snarling like enraged beasts and with their fangs out. Nick had the definite advantage in both strength and fighting ability, but River was desperate and his desperation made him as dangerous as a crazed bear.

As they crashed around the room, knocking the furniture about and throwing and dodging punches, River tried to think of a way to gain an advantage over Nick before Mina recovered enough to have a hand in their conflict. (Earlier, just in case of such a crisis as this, he'd hidden a second axe under the edge of the living room carpet, beside one of the windows. But at the moment he and Nick were too far from the weapon for it to do him any good.) Out of the corner of his eye, he noticed Mina staggering to her knees in the corridor. Nick's weird-looking weapon lay just inches from her feet, the light from the corridor's candles flickering ominously off its shiny steel.

He had no idea what that gun would do to him if Mina fired it at him, and had no desire to find out either. He could smell the result of the weapon's previous discharge—an unpleasant almost-citrus tang that hung in the house's musty air and refused to disperse.

But maybe Mina didn't know how to operate the weird weapon, because she didn't pick it up. Instead, to River's relief, she grabbed her wand up off the floor and headed towards him.

By now River was definitely losing the contest of strength against Nick. Nick had both hands wrapped around River's neck and was squeezing firmly. River was trying to return the violent favor, but with less success, his fingers finding less of a grip on the other man's neck. But Nick hadn't seen Mina approaching. As she reached them, River desperately attempted to swing Nick into her path, so she'd accidentally stun him with her wand.

But he discovered that Mina read his intent well. She ducked as he swung Nick towards her and instead of jabbing the wand into River's neck, kneed him in the groin instead.

That was it for River, the fight drained out of him like water through a colander. Nick let go of him and he fell back against the wall clutching his midriff, trying to breathe and groaning in pain simultaneously.

"The dumb bastard put up quite a fight," Nick said, wheezing. "Mina, get the freezer and let's get this finished with."

"Not so fast," an unfamiliar voice said then.

"Huh?" the vampires and River all said at once.

River straightened up and gaped at the living room doorway. Standing there were two odd black-garbed figures. They looked like ninjas. The shorter of the two figures had just picked up Nick's weird gun and was examining it.

Ninjas? Ninjas in West Virginia? River tried to get his head around that.

"Alright, freeze, you vampire punks," the ninja with the weird gun said, in a female voice with a distinctly American accent, a voice which River was certain he recognized from somewhere. "Yeah, freeze, vampire motherfuckers, before I freeze all of you."

CHAPTER 45

Crystal & Josie

"Yeah, freeze, vampire motherfuckers, before I freeze all of you!" Crystal felt really excited while saying this. She'd always wanted to talk tough like on TV, and now she thought she'd gotten it right.

"Be serious," Josie whispered.

They stepped fully into the living room. Across from them, the trio of vampires had momentarily abandoned their struggle and were staring at them with mixed expressions of anger and contempt. Crystal recognized Nick and Mina from their visits to the nightclub.

"Who the fuck are you?" Nick asked.

"Yeah," Mina agreed. "Who the hell are you two?"

"VEINS," Crystal promptly replied. "River is ours. As for you two vamp assholes, let's just say you picked a bad day to meddle in VEINS's business, or we picked a good one to meddle in yours. Now, we'll just—"

She didn't expect Nick to transform that fast. One moment, she was staring across the living room at a tall and muscular man, the next moment there was a massive wolf lunging at her.

Josie reacted faster, pulling out a stake and her mallet. The huge wolf changed direction and went for Josie. It sprang at Josie, who instantly dropped both stake and mallet and leapt up onto a couch to get out of its way. The couch was right beside a window and while moving, Josie inadvertently pulled the curtains open, revealing the cross painted on the window. At the sight of the cross, the wolf howled in fear and spun around. But as it turned, its muscular hindquarters rammed into Josie.

There was a loud shattering of glass and Josie vanished out of the window.

The wolf had in the meantime headed back for Crystal.

Crystal kept her nerve and pulled the trigger of the freezer gun. She was terrified that it wouldn't work and didn't know what to expect if it did work. She certainly didn't expect the gun to merely squirt out a pale bluish mist.

Fuck, I'm dead, she thought.

The wolf tried to dodge the blue spray, but failed. The mist covered the wolf.

"No!" Mina screamed, when the next moment, the wolf visibly shrunk, as if something was sucking its monstrous substance from it. The wolf remained exactly where it had been while trying to escape the mist, and in exactly the same position too—sitting back on its hind legs, with its forelimbs dangling in the air.

Crystal almost found the sight amusing, but Mina, with a look of intense anger on her face, was charging at her, the clear intent to kill Crystal in her eyes.

And Josie had fallen out of the window. Crystal didn't know if Josie was dead or alive.

Crystal swung the freezer gun up to blast Mina, but then Mina was shoved violently out of the way. Mina went clattering away out of sight behind Crystal. The freezer blast spilled over the wolf again.

Who . . . ? Crystal wondered in shock. But it was River, swinging an axe at the wolf. The axe smashed the frozen wolf right in the middle of its head, splitting it in two all the way down to the rug. The wolf fell apart in two halves that each hit the carpet with a dull clang.

"NOOOOOO!" Mina screamed from somewhere behind Crystal.

Crystal paid the vampire woman no attention. She'd just realized she was in the dominant position in this conflict. With Josie gone, she now had a chance to equalize things in her favor.

River was standing over the split wolf, a cold smile etched on his face.

"Just one left," he said quietly.

Crystal waited until River had lifted his head and was staring directly at her, then she hit him with the freezer spray.

She loved the look of shock on River's face when he realized what had happened. No!" he gasped in horror as the spray froze him stiff. Crystal had however remembered Dr. Xerxes instructions on freezing River. She'd concentrated the spray below his head, covering his chest, right arm and legs with it.

River shrunk just like the wolf had, quickly becoming emaciated. He tried to speak, but it was impossible.

"Damn, this stuff's really effective," Crystal said.

"I guess you think you're really cool, accomplishing all this," Mina's enraged voice said behind Crystal. "You think this makes you a real ninja, don't you!?"

Shit, I forgot Mina!

Crystal spun around to blast Mina too with the freezer spray. But the vampire woman was already right behind her and had a firm hold on her neck and head.

"Fuck, no!" Crystal screamed as Mina tore her head off her shoulders and flung it across the living room.

CHAPTER 46

Josie

Up in the branches of the ancient oak by the window, Josie took careful aim with the silver knife. She was wounded now. Being knocked out of the window by the wolf had both stunned her against one of the tree's giant boughs, and also broken her left forearm.

She wasn't about giving up yet, though. Not after seeing the callous way that Mina had torn Crystal's head off. That hurt Josie like she'd just been killed herself.

So, Josie took very careful aim with the silver knife. She'd crawled along the oak bough to be as near to the shattered window as she could manage without being noticed. At the moment she was right over the backup crew's black van.

Mina was standing right in front of River, who despite being frozen stiff, was somehow still on his feet.

"Well, River, looks like we got you anyway," Mina was saying. "Xerxes sure is going to be pleased to see you." Then she frowned. "But maybe we don't really need you alive anymore. We've already recovered your blood sample. I'd better call Xerxes and find out what he wants done with you."

Before Mina could pull out her phone, Josie flung her knife. One thing she didn't want was more vampires to deal with tonight. Not with her left arm broken and Crystal dead.

Josie Ottman never missed a knife throw from close range. She didn't miss this time either. The silver blade zipped through the air and buried itself to the hilt in Mina Cupples's neck.

Mina instantly froze in shock, flung her hands up to her neck, and screamed. And then her neck and head opened up like a door and hot ash began spilling out of her. River looked almost as surprised as Mina did at this completely unexpected and fatal turn of events.

"That one's for Crys. Rot in Hell, you vamp bitch," Josie growled at the disintegrating vampire woman, then she rolled sideways off the oak branch and with a loud and painful thump, fell on top of the parked backup van.

Fuck this! she thought, the pain in her shattered forearm almost making her scream.

***

After a short while Josie managed to get down from the top of the van, sliding forward over the windshield to the ground. Then, gripping her left arm tight to her body, she went inside the house to consider what to do.

First off, I need a doctor. And then . . . She had no idea what to do with River now. With her arm broken, she couldn't move him. *And even if I could move him, what do I do about storing him? Shit, if VEINS would simply get back to me now . . . And then, what am I gonna do about Crys's body too? Leave it here? . . . I'm gonna have to pack my bags and leave the state before the vamps come knocking at our door. That means I've got just till tomorrow night to get away. Fuck, I'd better call Jerry! He and Sheila can come pick me up . . . ! Shit, how could I have forgotten about them? We'll simply hide River in their garage until the HQ contacts us!*

While thinking this, Josie wandered into the downstairs living room. She winced at the gory mess that River had made of Olivia, then walked over to examine her corpse further. Almost immediately, her attention was caught by a slip of paper lying under Olivia's head. The paper had some writing on it that she couldn't make out. She bent over, closed Olivia's staring eyes, then tried to free the slip of paper. The slip didn't budge, so to work it loose, Josie bent Olivia's head sideways.

Then she heard a quiet click in the back of the couch.

Not knowing about the trap River had set here for the vampires, Josie's eyes widened with surprise.

Josie was even more surprised when the wooden spike shot out of its concealed vault in the back of the couch and impaled her completely through the neck, the stake's deadly predetermined course fatally ripping open both arteries and veins on both sides of her throat.

Josie Ottman collapsed to the living room floor and bled to death there, uncertain even of what had just killed her.

CHAPTER 47

River

River stood motionless in the darkened upstairs living room, unable to move his body. A human statue.

He could hardly speak, though the freezing began at his shoulders. He also found thinking difficult, as though whatever had frozen his body had slowed down his thought processes too.

Now and again his eyes went to one of the candles out in the corridor. And next, his gaze would flicker back inside, to the little piles of smoking ash that had been Mina and Nick.

And then, finally, his gaze would alight on the headless corpse of the 'ninja' girl, with blood spilled from her neck like a red star. River was certain he recognized her voice from somewhere. He knew he did. Who had she been?

He was defenseless now, property of whoever first found and claimed him. But would that be VEINS, or would it be the Vampire Society? Or would it happen to him that this freezing substance which held him so immobile would itself kill him? Or would he simply die of hunger and thirst?

Frozen as he was and helpless to help himself, all River could do was worry about his very uncertain future.

CHAPTER 48

Xerxes & the Vampire Society

"We've been trying to contact them for two hours now," Alexia King told her father. "It's clear that something has gone wrong with their mission. Or why else would we have lost all contact both with the posse and the human backup crew?"

Arnold Xerxes and the two vampires were in his office, still awaiting news from Nick and Mina.

Max King nodded. "Yes, it failed daughter, that's plain to see. River must have somehow defeated them and escaped."

"I think the bastard killed them all," Alexia said.

Xerxes nodded. Those were his exact thoughts: that Douglas River had killed everyone and then fled. He'd not voiced these impressions, of course, preferring to let the vampires reach their own conclusions.

"So what now, father?" Alexia asked. "Time is running out. We need to send out another strike team quickly. I'll lead this one if necessary."

"Oh, but we don't yet know where the last one ventured to," Max King said with a wry smile. "And put any thoughts of leading anything out of your head. About the only thing you're about leading, Alexia, is the doctor here down to the altar someday, if you can even manage that."

Alexia looked angry, then blushed. Xerxes looked embarrassed.

"But enough about your activities behind my back," the old vampire went on. "I don't like losing people over this. I'm not sending out any more vampires after Douglas River and that's that."

189

Xerxes felt he should say something. "But, sir, Alexia has a point. We do need to neutralize River and quickly too."

Alexia nodded. Her father shook his head. "Only when we're certain we'll get the job done right. We can't have any more failures." He lifted a finger to make a point. "And also, the more people we involve in this, the more people who know about it. With what's at stake here, it will be extremely unwise to let what we know get to the wrong ears." He pierced Xerxes with his steely ancient gaze. By my count, we've lost ten high-profile vampires in just one week; some of those, national figures. I think it's time we retreat and regroup."

"He may already be turning toxic on us," Xerxes said.

"And he may not be," Max King calmly replied. "We don't know for sure either way."

"But, father—"

"I'm not saying we're giving up the hunt, Alexia. Yes, Xerxes will continue to work on the blood sample we recovered to develop a cure for humanitis. But I must think. I must put all my mental energies into figuring out a proper solution to this mess, before it becomes too big a mess to control. Like I said, we can't have any more failures."

"Actually, we might never need that cure anyway, father."

Max King looked at his daughter. "How do you mean, Alexia?"

She explained: "Well, River is only toxic to us vampires if he comes in contact with us before the disease destroys him." She looked at Xerxes for confirmation. "Am I right, honey?"

Xerxes nodded. "Yes, that's what the books all say."

"So then, why don't we just make a point of avoiding him? We'll leave him alone to rot in peace." She smiled coldly. "Just as I suspect that River himself will make a point of avoiding us too from now on."

"I believe I see your point," Xerxes said. "It's a damn good one."

Alexia shrugged. "Might work, I guess."

"No," Max King told them both, shaking his head emphatically. "Unfortunately, we *can't* forget about River." He frowned. "Oh, don't get me wrong: I would just *love* to do what Alexia has suggested, and hope the problem would take care of itself. But there remains the danger that River may contact other vampires who don't know he's fallen out of favor and spread his infection to them also."

Alexia frowned too. "Yes, there is that to consider. I hadn't thought of that."

"Alright, we'll decide fully tomorrow night," Max King said. "By then we should have enough information to plan well, maybe even sufficient information to justify sending out yet another search posse after our fugitive. And for the moment, I'll postpone my trip to Chicago. I want to personally keep an eye on matters here."

"I'll take over running the Haven club," Alexia said, a fire in her green eyes. "Is this okay with you, daddy?"

Her father looked from her to Xerxes, then he smiled. This time his smile was warm, bright as the sunlight he'd not seen for two millennia. "Alright, you can, so long as you promise not to set up any posses to go searching for River behind my back." He nodded at Xerxes. "You keep an eye on her."

Xerxes bowed. "To the utmost of my ability, sir."

Max King smiled coldly. "And if Nick and Mina are actually deceased, then we need to reorder our security setup. But that's a job for my next nighttime awakening. Now my old bones need to get some sleep. But a drink first." He nodded to Xerxes. "Have your charming secretary serve us, please."

Xerxes pressed the buzzer to summon Mildred.

River will return in *Icarus.*

A Vampire's Nightmare Continues . . .

RIVER
BOOK 2 ICARUS

GARY LEE VINCENT

ABOUT THE AUTHOR

Gary Lee Vincent was born in Clarksburg, West Virginia and is an accomplished author, musician, actor, producer, director and entrepreneur. In 2010, his horror novel *Darkened Hills* was selected as 2010 Book of the Year winner by *Foreword Reviews Magazine* and became the pilot novel for *DARKENED - THE WEST VIRGINIA VAMPIRE SERIES*, that encompasses the novels *Darkened Hills, Darkened Hollows, Darkened Waters, Darkened Souls, Darkened Minds* and *Darkened Destinies*. He has also authored the bizarro thriller *Passageway*, a tribute to H.P. Lovecraft, and *When the Bedposts Shake*, an erotic horror.

Gary co-authored the novel *Belly Timber* with John Russo, Solon Tsangaras, Dustin Kay and Ken Wallace, and co-authored the novel *Attack of the Melonheads* with Bob Gray and Solon Tsangaras.

As an actor, Gary has appeared in over seventy feature films and multiple television series, including *House of Cards, Mindhunter, The Walking Dead,* and *Stranger Things*.

As a director, Gary got his directorial debut with *A Promise to Astrid*. He has also directed the films *Desk Clerk, Dispatched*, and the 2020 remake of John Russo's iconic horror film *Midnight*.

WHEN THE BEDPOSTS SHAKE

AN EROTIC TERROR

GARY LEE VINCENT

WHEN THE BEDPOSTS SHAKE
(RING OF THE SUCCUBUS)

Jack Crannson was having a midlife crisis. A successful architect, Jack was more interest in running his business than saving his marriage. With his workaholic wife fueling his own disinterest, he decides to move closer to his work by purchasing an older house in the Maple Lake section of Bridgeport, West Virginia.

The house purchase seemed like a logical enough choice for Jack, despite Samantha, his estranged wife's, protest. The only illogical thing was the condition that came with the house from Mr. Bannering, the home's previous owner. . .

Mr. Bannering warned that Jack mustn't use the north bedroom, and under no circumstances, sleep in the bed. It was locked and needed to stay that way.

What Mr. Bannering failed to disclose was that trapped within that room was a demonic force, a she-devil succubus named Cali that was looking for some way to escape her prison and enter the earthly realm in the flesh to prey on male victims by feeding on their sexual energy. With the house having a new owner, she may just get her wish.

Warning: this novel contains language intended for an adult audience.

2010 Book of the Year WINNER
ForeWord Reviews Magazine

DARKENED HILLS

GARY LEE VINCENT

DARKENED HILLS
DARKENED – THE WEST VIRGINIA VAMPIRE SERIES
Book I by Gary Lee Vincent

"2010 Book of the Year WINNER"
- Foreword Reviews Magazine

A tale of gripping psychological horror!

When evil descends on a small West Virginia town, who will survive?

Jonathan did not start out his life to become a rambler, it just worked out that way. William was a troubled youth with something to hide. Both were from Melas, a small town tucked away in the West Virginia hills... a town where disappearances are happening more and more frequently.

After the suicide of a wanted serial killer, the townsfolk thought the nightmare was over. But when a centuries-old vampire is discovered they find out the hard way it's just getting started.

Dark secrets can only stay hidden for so long and when the devil comes to collect, there will be hell to pay. Can Jonathan and William find a way to stop the vampire before it's too late? Find out in Darkened Hills!

Darkened Hills is a gothic vampire novel written in the spirit of Dracula with much more sinister characters and eroticism then the old Victorian classic.

For series information, visit **www.DarkenedHills.com**.

www.ingramcontent.com/pod-product-compliance
Lightning Source LLC
Chambersburg PA
CBHW070929250626
47159CB00009B/3171